Shadows of
GUILT

ANNE SCHRAFF

SADDLEBACK
EDUCATIONAL PUBLISHING

A Boy Called Twister

Dark Secrets

Deliverance

The Fairest

If You Really Loved Me

Leap of Faith

Like a Broken Doll

The Lost

No Fear

One of Us

Outrunning the Darkness

The Quality of Mercy

Shadows of Guilt

The Stranger

Time of Courage

To Be a Man

To Catch a Dream

The Unforgiven

The Water's Edge

Wildflower

SADDLEBACK
EDUCATIONAL PUBLISHING
www.sdlback.com

ISBN-13: 978-1-61651-001-5
ISBN-10: 1-61651-001-3
eBook: 978-1-60291-786-6

Printed in Guangzhou, China
0411/04-76-11

15 14 13 12 11   3 4 5 6 7

CHAPTER ONE

What was *that*?" Jaris Spain screamed. He was working the late shift at the Chicken Shack when a noise that sounded like gunfire exploded from Pequot Street a block away.

"Probably just a car backfiring, bro," Trevor Jenkins said. He was Jaris's best friend, and at the moment he was eating a chicken nugget.

Jaris turned cold. He knew what backfiring sounded like. "Trev! Somebody's shooting over there!" he exclaimed. Once, when he was six or seven, Jaris was coming home from a movie with his father. A car drove by and a woman was shot. Pop covered Jaris's eyes but too late. Jaris had seen the blood on the woman's white sweater. Nothing else sounded quite like gunfire, and he knew he had just heard it from Pequot Street.

Within seconds, the eerie whine of emergency vehicles drowned out the normal noises of the night. Jaris grabbed his cell phone and called home. "Mom, I'm okay. But something bad just happened over on Pequot. I heard gunfire and now there's sirens. I'll be coming home right away."

Pop must have grabbed the phone from Mom after he saw the shocked look on her face. "Jaris, what's going down?" he asked.

"Shooting over on Pequot, Pop. I'm okay. I'm getting off work in a few minutes," Jaris explained.

"Listen to me boy. Sit tight. I don't want you walking home, you got it? I'm coming in the pickup to get you," Pop commanded.

It was only a few blocks from the Chicken Shack to Jaris's house. He easily walked the distance on a normal day. "Okay, Pop," he replied. "You got it."

Jaris turned to Trevor, who lived on the same street as Jaris. "Man, there's room in Pop's pickup for the both of us," Jaris said.

"Your father's coming?" Trevor asked, wide-eyed.

"Yeah. Who knows what that gunfire's all about man. Maybe the gangs are making war on each other," Jaris said.

"Or maybe some fool's shooting a stray cat off a fence," Trevor countered. "Seems like everybody's got a gun around here."

More sirens wailed in the darkness. Jaris had a terrible feeling in the pit of his stomach. Somebody was hurt—or worse. Maybe it was somebody he knew. Jaris grew up in this neighborhood. He knew most of the kids, most of the families. The gangbangers generally lived south of Grant Avenue, and their violence didn't spill over into Jaris's neighborhood. But the gunfire came from Pequot Street, several blocks north of Grant.

Pop pulled up in his green pickup. Jaris and Trevor piled in. "Bad business," Pop growled.

"Did you hear anything about the shooting on the radio, Pop?" Jaris asked.

"Just about heavy traffic around Pequot due to a police action," Pop answered.

"Maybe the cops were chasing somebody and there was a shootout," Trevor suggested.

"I'll just be glad to get you guys home," Pop said. "Your mom is a freakin' nervous wreck and your mom too, Trev."

When Pop pulled into the Spain driveway, Trevor jumped out and ran across the street to his house. The front door of the Spain house opened, and Mom was framed there, a terrible look on her face. "It's Maya Archer," Mom cried. "She was shot!"

Jaris's brain went into a spin. Thirteen-year-old Maya, Sami's little sister? Sami was a junior at Tubman High School too, and she was one of Jaris's best friends. Who would want to shoot a little girl like Maya?

"Maya was coming out of the deli, and she was caught in the gunfire," Mom said. "Dear God, what is this world coming to?" Mom groaned.

"Is she okay, Mom?" Jaris asked, his breath coming in a gasp. Sami was always talking about her little sister, her off-the-wall jokes, her dancing. Maya was friends with Jaris's fourteen-year-old sister Chelsea.

"I don't know," Mom sighed. She appeared near tears. "She's been taken to the hospital."

Chelsea was standing alongside Mom, her face red from crying. "Jaris! They shot Maya!" she sobbed.

"Come on," Pop said. "We're going to the hospital. Maya must be down at Drew Emergency."

Jaris and Chelsea hurried toward their father.

"No," Mom protested. "Maybe those shooters are still out there looking for trouble. It's dangerous to be driving around tonight.

You guys need to stay home until the police catch the shooters."

"We're going," Pop insisted harshly. "If it was one of our kids shot like Maya, Lonnie and Mattie Archer would be there for us, and you know that, Monie."

"We gotta go, Mom!" Jaris sided with his father. "It's Sami's little sister!"

"Maya is one of my best friends," Chelsea cried. "I want to go!"

"Lorenzo," Mom pleaded with her husband. "There's nothing you guys can do. The doctors and nurses are helping Maya and—"

"Come on, you kids," Pop snapped. "We're going!"

"All right," Mom said. "I'll go too. We can use my car. I'm not sitting here alone in this house worrying myself sick about you, afraid that those criminals are shooting at my husband and kids!" Mom pulled on a sweater against the evening chill. In a few minutes they were driving toward Drew Emergency Hospital.

"I know what it's like sitting in an emergency room, waiting to find out if somebody you love is dead or alive," Pop explained. "I went through it with both my parents. It felt like I was sitting in that blasted waiting room forever before a doctor came to tell me what was going on. Right now Lonnie and Mattie are going through hell and they need us."

"It must have been a stray shot that hit Maya," Jaris suggested. "Nobody would have shot her on purpose."

"Jacklyn's mother called me right after it happened. Jacklyn Webster. Jacklyn and Keisha and Maya had just finished cheerleader practice, and they stopped at the deli for one of those big colas they were going to split. A lot of kids from Tubman High were there. Marko Lane and DeWayne Pike were coming out just ahead of the girls," Mom told them.

Marko Lane was a creep, but Jaris didn't think he was mixed up with gangs. DeWayne Pike was a good guy. He had just finished playing Charles Darnay in Tubman's presentation of *A Tale of Two Cities*. Jaris had played Sydney Carton.

"Maybe it was just random," Pop figured. "Maybe they saw a bunch of kids and they just let loose. They don't need a reason. Some of them initiate new gang members by asking them to do a shooting. I'd like to get my hands on them for five minutes. They wouldn't be blasting away at kids after I got through with them." Pop was furious, and Jaris couldn't blame him. To think that a sweet little girl like Maya just wanted a cola and ended up being shot was horrifying.

They parked in the lot for the emergency visitors, and the four of them rushed to the waiting room.

"That's Lonnie Archer's van," Pop pointed out. "I recognize it. We took it when he and I went fishing at Arrowhead."

When Jaris and his family got to the waiting room, they saw Sami and her parents. Sami was a big, tough girl with a soft heart, but right now her eyes were red from crying. Mom went to Mattie Archer and gave her a big hug. Pop embraced Lonnie Archer, and Jaris and Chelsea both put their arms around Sami. The Archers had two children, Sami and Maya. The girls were their whole life.

A young Asian doctor stepped into the waiting room. "The Archers?" he called out. Lonnie and Mattie rushed over to him. "Your daughter is out of surgery," he announced. "She's in the recovery room. She did well. The bullet struck her in the thigh, and her femur was broken, so that has been repaired and she received a blood transfusion. You'll be able to see her in about one hour. She'll recover completely from the injury with physical therapy."

Lonnie and Mattie Archer, with Sami between them, laughed and cried. They praised God and praised the doctors. The Spains joined in the celebration. Then Mattie Archer wept and said, "Monie, Lorenzo, you guys were here for us. We'll never forget that. You guys are the best. Jaris, Chelsea, you're like our babies too!"

"Nobody could have kept us away," Pop said. "Our kids started school together Mattie. And before I got my job with Jackson at the garage, Lonnie, you got me a part-time job with the sanitation department, and that kept us going." Pop looked over at Mom with a half smile, "Remember, Monie? Those were the days you were still in college, learning to be a big shot teacher. If it hadn't of been for the Archers, we wouldn't have had fried chicken and dumplings on the table."

Mom smiled sheepishly. "Yeah, we were up against it all right."

Sami huddled with Jaris and Chelsea. "When I heard that Maya got shot, it was like my heart stopped," Sami said. "I got all cold and I thought I was dying. I couldn't breathe. I thought she was dead. I swear, I thought I was gonna die. We were expecting her home with Keisha and Jacklyn in a little while, and then we got this call that

Maya was shot and I thought I was losin' my little sister. I couldn't stand to lose her. I was three years old when she was born, and I loved that child from the minute I saw her. She's the best little sister in the whole world."

The Spains stayed at the hospital until Maya's parents went in to see their daughter in the intensive care unit. Then the Spains headed home. It was almost midnight.

"The Archers got a lot of good friends, but nobody but us came," Pop commented.

"Not everybody knew what happened," Mom said. "And it's scary to be out in the dark when there's been a shooting. You can't blame people for being scared. It wasn't about not caring. It was about fear."

"It's about being a friend," Pop insisted. "Times like this, you need friends to stand by you. Can't let anything stop you." Jaris could hear pride in his father's voice that he insisted they come. A lot of times Mom overrode Pop's decisions and that cut him down. Jaris could see the damage it did.

But this time he wasn't going to let that happen. He was not going to let his friends down, not tonight, with their child's life maybe hanging in the balance.

"I hope they catch the people who shot Maya," Mom said. "Those gangs are so evil."

"It's hard for the police to catch those drive-by shooters," Jaris remarked. "People see them and know who they are, but they're scared to tell. Or maybe they know the guys and don't want to get them in trouble."

"It's so awful that it happened at the deli," Chelsea chimed in. "We've always felt safe there."

Pop turned around and gave Chelsea a hard look. "No more hanging around there or anywhere else at night, or even close to dark, baby," he dictated the order.

"Maybe Mom is right," Jaris's mother added. "Maybe this neighborhood is just getting too dangerous." Grandma Jessie, Mom's mother, was always urging the Spains to move to a better neighborhood. But Pop had a good job nearby at Jackson's

Auto Repair, and Jaris and Chelsea didn't want to leave their schools and their friends.

"Bad stuff happens all over," Pop argued. "Couple of college students were walking outside their nice, ritzy campus, and a drunk driver killed them. Big baseball rookie, a kid with a great future, gets killed in a hit-and-run accident. You can't let fear run your life. It's okay to take precautious, like having our kids staying away from the deli at night, but we got a good neighborhood here. We got good friends. There's no need to flee from our home."

"I just see the graffiti getting closer," Mom remarked. "I don't know. When something like this happens it makes you wonder."

"You know what?" Chelsea said. "Me and Maya's other friends from school are going to the hospital tomorrow to see her. We'll make cute cards and bring her a stuffed animal. She likes meerkats. We'll get her a meerkat."

"Sounds great, chili pepper," Jaris said.

When they got home, Jaris went to his bedroom and called Trevor. "I guess you heard, Trev. It was Sami's little sister got shot. Maya," Jaris told him.

"Yeah. Keisha's mom called my mom," Trevor responded. "You know what the buzz is? The shot was meant for DeWayne Pike," Trevor added. "The girls were right behind him and that's how Maya got shot."

"No way!" Jaris gasped. "DeWayne is about as far from being a gang member as I am! That's crazy." Jaris worked with DeWayne and Sereeta Prince on the play just weeks ago. Until this happened, Jaris was riding high from all the good reviews he got playing Sydney Carton. DeWayne got equally good notices for playing Charles Darnay. DeWayne didn't seem to have any problems that would make someone want to shoot him. "Trevor, that just doesn't make any sense," Jaris said.

"I thought the same thing, Jare, but listen up. Jacklyn Webster is telling everybody she and Keisha and Maya were right behind DeWayne. He stood still for a minute just outside the place. Keisha goes, 'Hey DeWayne, you're a better door than a window. Get out of the way.' Just then this car slows down . . . and DeWayne drops down, like taking cover. And the shots rang out. Like everybody is thinking DeWayne got hit, 'cause it all happened so fast. Y'-hear what I'm saying? It's like when he saw the car, he hit the dirt. Like he expected something. Now the girls behind him were in the line of fire and Maya took a shot . . . "

Jaris frowned. "Yeah okay, that's weird. Maybe DeWayne sees the car slow down, and he's just a cautious guy and he gets out of the way," Jaris suggested.

"Man unless you think you got an enemy out there, you don't see a car slow down and go for cover," Trevor insisted.

After he talked to Trevor, Jaris tried to think if anything about DeWayne Pike seemed suspicious. His family moved to the neighborhood a few years ago. He started at Tubman High in the ninth grade. His family was from Florida, and both parents were professional people. DeWayne was a good actor. He was involved in the drama department at Tubman since his freshman year. DeWayne dressed well and drove a silver Honda. He never seemed to lack money for stuff he wanted. Nothing about him was sinister.

At Tubman High the next day, the shooting was on everybody's mind. Alonee Lennox, one of Jaris's good friends, came running over when she saw Jaris. "Jaris," she told him, "my mom and dad went to the hospital this morning to see Maya. Mom made the Archers a casserole too. It's so awful what happened."

"We were at the hospital last night," Jaris said. "Poor Sami took it really hard. I don't think we'll see her in school today."

"No," Alonee objected, "there she is."

Jaris and Alonee both hurried over to give Sami a hug.

"Maya doing fine this morning," Sami announced. "I didn't feel like coming to school, but then I figured everybody gonna want to know how she's doin', and I'm here to say the Good Lord spared my little sister. Hallelujah! She gonna have some tough rehab now, 'cause the bone was broken in her thigh. Gonna break that girl's heart to have to drop dancing and cheerleading and to have to hobble around on crutches, but she's gonna make it and be good as new. Whoever did this, I hope they get him and put him in jail for thirty years! To shoot a little girl like that!"

Suddenly, Trevor was standing there. "Some people are saying the shooter was after DeWayne Pike," he suggested.

Sami spun around. "What you talkin' about dude?" she demanded. Sami was in the play too, and she worked well with DeWayne. Everybody did. He was a very nice guy.

"I don't know, Sami," Trevor said, "but it seems like Maya got the shot intended for him."

"I heard that Marko Lane was in the deli too," Alonee interjected. "Maybe somebody was shooting at him. He's got a lot of enemies. I still think it was just a random shooting."

"Jacklyn Webster is saying DeWayne ducked when the car slowed down. He did that before the shooting," Trevor explained. "That's what she's saying."

"Kids get things mixed up," Sami argued. "I mean, like when something like that happens, it's hard for witnesses to remember what happened first."

At lunchtime, Jaris called Chelsea on her cell. He asked her if Jacklyn was in school. "Yeah, she and Keisha are right here eating lunch with me," Chelsea said. Jaris asked to talk to Keisha, and Chelsea gave her phone to her. "Keisha," Jaris asked, "did you see DeWayne Pike drop down before the shots were fired at the deli last night?"

"I don't know, Jaris. Seems like he did," Keisha answered, "but maybe it was after the shots . . . I'm just not sure."

Jacklyn took the phone then. She seemed to know what Jaris had asked Keisha. "That boy, he went down before anybody started shooting," she asserted.

"You sure, Jacklyn?" Jaris asked.

"Jaris, I saw that play about the French at your school. I saw it two times 'cause I got a crush on DeWayne playing that Charles Darnay. I was looking right at him last night and I know what I seen," Jacklyn stated firmly.

They ended the call, and Jaris put the phone down. He sat there bewildered. It didn't make sense that somebody was shooting at DeWayne Pike. It just didn't make sense.

CHAPTER TWO

In Mr. Pippin's English class, Marko Lane, ever ready to distract the nervous teacher from his lecture, raised his hand.

"Yes?" Mr. Pippin nodded toward Marko. "Do you have a question about the Hemingway story?"

"No," Marko said. "I just wondered if you heard about the little gangbanger girl getting shot at the deli last night, right over on Pequot Street."

Jaris felt his skin turn hot with rage. "Maya Archer is not a gangbanger. She's a great kid from a good family. She was an innocent victim," he snarled in a seething voice.

Mr. Pippin looked stricken, as he always did when he realized he had lost his class. "Yes, well, it was a terrible thing and let's all hope the police find the culprits quickly," the teacher said, hoping to get back to Hemingway. "Now, about the story we have all just read—"

Marko ignored the teacher. "Car full of rival gangbangers probably were the shooters. The Nite Ryders are one gang, but there're others. They don't like to see other gangs tagging their space."

"I hear," another girl chimed in, "there was a big fight at the middle school between some Nite Ryder chicks from Grant Avenue and some girls from the Red X. They were pulling each other's hair, then one girl got on her cell and called her boyfriend, and that's when the shooting started."

"That never happened," Jaris objected.

Marko turned to Jaris. "What do you know? You think you're such a big shot 'cause you were in that stupid play. You want to know something Spain? You stunk in that play. The play stunk too. Everybody hated it. It was bor-r-ring. Who cares about a bunch of Frenchmen chopping heads off a thousand years ago?" Wild laughter from Marko's friends followed.

"Please!" Mr. Pippin's thin voice rose almost to a scream, "We have read this short story, "A Canary for One," by Ernest Hemingway—a very simple story, but one that—"

"'Tweet-tweet,' said the canary," Marko Lane sang, giving rise to another round of laughter.

"The basic conflict in the story," Mr. Pippin was shouting now over the buzz in the room. He was red in the face. "The theme of the story . . . the theme . . . "

Marko threw back his head, laughing. "Maybe the old fool will bust a gut," he roared.

"Oh man," Jaris said when the class was over, "I sure wish Mr. Pippin would take a vacation or something."

"Yeah," Alonee agreed, "or Marko Lane and his buddies would get expelled!"

Just then Jaris noticed DeWayne Pike walking with Sereeta. Since they'd acted in the play together, they had gotten closer. In the play, DeWayne as Charles Darnay was married to Sereeta's Lucie. They had some good love scenes in the play, and now those scenes were spilling over into their real lives. Their going together bothered Jaris because, before the play, he and Sereeta were closer than they had ever been.

"Hi you guys," Alonee called out as the couple came close. "How're you doing, DeWayne? That must have been awful last night."

"Yeah. I'll tell you, I didn't get much sleep last night. I've never been so close to gunfire in my life, and I hope I never am again," DeWayne responded.

"I bet you talked to the police for a long time," Jaris said. "I mean, you were right in the middle of it. You must have seen poor little Maya go down."

"The police asked me a lot of questions, but I'm afraid I wasn't much help," DeWayne replied. "I wasn't looking into the street when the car came along, so I couldn't even tell them the kind of car it was. The first I knew that something was wrong was when I heard the shots and then a girl's scream. Man that was really awful. It was surreal. Man I never thought I'd be near anything like that. Where I lived in Florida, there weren't any gangs. A few alligators would come up from the swamps, but they didn't bother me. I'm glad the girl is doing okay. Sami said she'll be fine. That's really great."

"One of Maya Archer's friends said you seemed to duck and hit the ground even before the shooting started," Jaris suggested. "She said it was like you saw something coming."

DeWayne Pike's expression changed. He stared at Jaris with an almost hostile look. He had dark, intense eyes in his handsome face, and now they seemed on fire. He cleared his throat and turned to Sereeta. "See you after biology, Sereeta."

"Yeah, maybe we can study together," Sereeta said, heading for the biology classroom. Now Jaris and Alonee were alone with DeWayne.

"What are you trying to say, Jaris? I mean, that really came out of left field," DeWayne asked in a cold voice. "That I knew there would be a shooting even before it happened and I ducked?"

"I'm just telling you what this girl who was with Maya said," Jaris stated. He was feeling uneasy under DeWayne's icy glare.

"Alonee," DeWayne asked, turning to her, "what's going on here?"

"I don't know what you mean DeWayne," Alonee said. She seemed nervous too.

"Jaris, since we finished the play, Sereeta and I have been seeing each other a lot. Maybe that doesn't sit so well with you," DeWayne suggested. "I know you like Sereeta too, and maybe you think I've been moving on your girl. But she's not your girl. I can understand that you're ticked off that maybe she's not interested in you . . . but I resent this little game of yours to make me look bad. Like I knew the shots were coming and I looked out for my own hide and let the girls behind me get hit."

"DeWayne," Jaris said, forcing his voice to be calm, "this has nothing to do with how I feel about Sereeta. I was shocked when Jacklyn Webster said what she did. I didn't know what to make of it."

"Well, I can help you out there," DeWayne insisted. "What you can make of it is this: When I heard the shots, I hit the ground. It was a reflex action. Self-preservation. This girl, she got mixed up. In all the shock and terror of those minutes, she got confused. Anybody would be terrified and confused, but she's a kid—thirteen? She was in the middle of a hail of bullets. She sees her friend go down bleeding. And the kid got it all mixed up. That's what you can make of it, Jaris."

"Okay." Jaris accepted the explanation.

"And one more thing, Jaris. You were a very good Sydney Carton in the play.

Everybody said you were the most powerful actor in the play. You can be proud of that. But don't forget, even in the play, Carton didn't get the girl. Charles Danay did. The guy I was playing. So be a good sport, Spain. If Sereeta likes somebody else more than she likes you, let it go."

Jaris didn't say anything as DeWayne strode away. Alonee reached out and touched Jaris's arm. "I know you well enough to be sure you would never try to use something like the shooting to make a rival look bad. You're too good a person to do that. I'm sorry DeWayne took it like that," Alonee assured him.

"Yeah well, what are you gonna do? All I know is that Jacklyn Webster is so sure about what she saw," Jaris objected. "Then again, that doesn't make it true. It's easy to be sure about things that aren't true."

Jaris decided he would drop the issue. He didn't want to make an enemy of DeWayne. He didn't want it to get back to Sereeta that Jaris was trying to make trouble for DeWayne just because they both liked her. Maybe, Jaris thought, Jacklyn *did* get mixed up about the sequence of events that night.

The following day, Trevor, Sami, and Alonee went to see Maya in the hospital. Maya was a pretty little girl who took after her lean father. Sami was big, like her mother. Maya was sitting up in bed, holding the stuffed meerkat that Chelsea and her other friends had given her. But she looked anything but happy.

"I got an old pin in my leg where it was broken," Maya murmured darkly. "And I'm missing cheerleading and my dance class and *everything*."

Sami gave her little sister a hug. "That's okay baby. You'll be fine. When Daddy was in that big Gulf War, a big bomb went off and busted both his legs, and now he does just fine," she told her sister.

Jaris added, "It won't make a bit of difference sweetheart. You can still be a ballerina and, before that, the best cheerleader in the world."

Maya smiled at Jaris. "You're cute. I came to see you in the play, and I cried when you got killed. I thought you were so brave," she admitted.

"When you goin' home, Maya?" Trevor asked.

"Tomorrow, but I gotta have crutches, nasty old crutches." Maya wrinkled up her nose. "I hate those gang members who shot me. I hate them like everything!"

"Don't waste time hatin' anybody, darlin'," Sami said. "It just makes you feel worse. They'll get what's coming to them."

"Chelsea says she'll carry my backpack for me at school," Maya mentioned, "and Jacklyn and Keisha are gonna get my lunch and stuff."

"Child, you gonna be treated like a queen," Sami said.

"You got really nice friends," Jaris remarked. "That tells me you're a special girl."

A thoughtful look came to Maya's face then, almost a troubled look. "Mama says those bad men wanted to shoot somebody

29

else and they shot me by mistake," she told them. "Do you think they wanted to shoot Marko Lane? He's really mean. He makes horrible jokes about people and hurts them. Like he'll see an old man and he makes fun of how he walks. He even makes fun of kids. Keisha has a lot of braids, and he calls her 'piggy head' and one time she cried."

"I think those guys were just shooting and they didn't care who got hit," Jaris offered. "They saw a bunch of kids and they just fired."

"Don't they like kids?" Maya asked.

Jaris shrugged. "Maybe not kids over on Pequot Street. Gangbangers get mad at people from another side of town. It's like war, when you hate the other guys because they got a different flag," Jaris explained.

"I know a gangbanger," Maya said.

Jaris, Trevor, and Sami looked at one another cautiously. "Come on baby," Sami objected, "you don't know any gangbangers."

"I do too," Maya insisted. "I was skateboarding and this boy was painting stuff on a fence with a spray can. He was making big, puffy letters. It was kind of pretty. I asked him what he was doing, and he said he was marking off turf. He said he belonged to a gang and this was their turf. He said he was a Nite Ryder. He wasn't mean or anything."

Sami looked alarmed. "Baby, you oughtn't to be talkin' to strangers like that. You know better than that. Don't you do that anymore, you hear what I'm sayin'?" she demanded.

"I won't, Sami. But he was nice. He gave me a butterfly pin," Maya answered.

"Did he tell you his name?" Jaris asked.

"Not a real name. He just told me people called him Sparky," Maya replied.

As they walked down to the elevators leading from the hospital, Jaris told the others, "Maya was talking to a dropout from Tubman, Shane Burgess. He was a great baseball player at Tubman before he got derailed. I don't think he's hardcore gang, just a wannabe. But still, Maya shouldn't be talking to any strangers."

"You can say that again," Sami agreed.

Coming from the other direction and waiting for an elevator going up was the Webster family, including Jacklyn. They carried a big "Get Well" balloon. Jaris didn't know the family well, but he had seen Jacklyn at Chelsea's sleepovers.

"Maya's doing fine," Sami told them. "She's goin' home tomorrow on crutches. She ain't too jazzed about that."

"Oh goody," Jacklyn said. "I miss her so much. I hope she comes back to school real soon. School isn't as much fun when she's not there." Jacklyn paused then and looked at Jaris and Sami. "Did that boy say why he fell down before the gun was fired?" she asked.

Mrs. Webster frowned. "Jacklyn keeps telling that story," she said. "She says there was this boy at the door and he dropped down before the shots were fired, like he knew what was coming. Jacklyn says that's why Maya got hit. He got out of the way."

Jaris met Mrs. Webster's gaze. "I talked

to the guy, DeWayne Pike. He said it never happened that way. He said he ducked when he heard the shots."

"You see, Jacklyn?" Mrs. Webster scolded. "You just got mixed up. I'm not blaming you. When something awful like that happens, we get all rattled. We don't know what came first and what came second."

Just before the Websters got on the elevator to the third floor, Jacklyn ran to Jaris. She had large, expressive eyes. She whispered to Jaris, who was the closest to her of the three teenagers. "I didn't get mixed up. I didn't!" Then Jacklyn ran to get on the elevator with her parents.

Jaris couldn't get the deadly serious look on the girl's face out of his mind. What bothered him most of all was that Sereeta was spending so much time with DeWayne lately. If something in DeWayne's past made him a target for shooters, then Sereeta at his side could be in danger too. That possibility haunted Jaris.

Jaris's father had exaggerated fears and dark moods, and Jaris thought that his Pop's tendencies might be in his genes. Maybe, Jaris thought, he was putting too much stock in Jacklyn's story. Maybe he was, as Pop often did, seeing things in the worst possible light.

Jaris's father often relived his disappointments, like his inability to afford college and become a scientist instead of an auto mechanic. Sometimes Jaris's parents quarreled over his bad moods. But Pop helped Jaris a lot in getting the role of Sydney Carton in *A Tale of Two Cities*, and that cooperation seemed to lift Pop's spirits. There wasn't as much quarreling at home.

But now, as Jaris came home, he felt the old tension in the house. His parents were arguing again. Jaris thought there was trouble at Jackson's Auto Repair. That always put him in a bad mood. Or maybe Pop had fallen into his old habit of stopping off after work for a few drinks at his favorite bar. Mom hated when he came home after doing that.

But it wasn't any of those things. Jaris's parents were arguing over Ms. McDowell, Jaris's favorite teacher, who made American history come alive as nobody at Tubman High had ever seen it.

"As usual," Mom reported crisply, "your father and I don't agree on an important issue."

"Your mother thinks we need to make trouble for Ms. McDowell, your history teacher, and I think we need to mind our own business and leave her alone," Pop added.

"Ms. McDowell?" Jaris gasped. "She's the best teacher at Tubman, Mom. What's going on?"

"Jaris, I *know* she's a wonderful teacher," Mom agreed. "But she has this delinquent brother and she's opened her home to him. He now lives with her in her apartment, and, well, he has gang connections, and that means her home becomes a hangout for all sorts of dubious characters. I just think it's unhealthy for a teacher at Tubman High to be harboring a boy with gang ties.

I've always known about the brother and I sympathized with how she tried to help him when he was a ninth grader, but now he's a hardened miscreant."

Pop laughed harshly. "Only your uppity mother would use the word 'miscreant.' A poor kid who took a wrong path, and now his sister is trying to help him and he's a miscreant!" he mocked.

"I happen to think Ms. McDowell is enabling her brother to continue his criminal ways," Mom insisted stubbornly.

"'Enabling,' " Pop said. "Another educational psych word. We used to call it being there for your family even if they weren't up to snuff. In my day we called that loving your family members and holding out your hand to them to lift them up when they stumbled. Like that Robert Frost poem—I forget the title—about helping someone in trouble."

"The Death of the Hired Man," Jaris said. At last Jaris was getting some benefit from being in Mr. Pippin's class. He had read the poem for that class.

"Yeah, yeah," Pop said eagerly. "I remember the line 'Home is the place where, when you have to go there, they have to take you in.' Something like that." Pop smiled gratefully at Jaris for remembering the poem. "So this kid, he has no place to go. He has no home. But his sister has a home and he goes there, and you want his family to toss him out. Just because he's not some little goody-two-shoes kid, he oughta be kicked in the can."

Mom rolled her eyes. "Oh Lorenzo, give me a break," she pleaded. "I had no problem when Ms. McDowell helped a little fourteen-year-old—but this guy is now street smart and tough. He's been in a gang. He's done drugs. I think somebody needs to tell Torie McDowell that her brother belongs in a good group home for boys like him."

"Hey, I got an idea," Pop said in a sarcastic voice. "Why don't you form a committee, Monie? You and that stuffed shirt principal at your school—Greg Maynard. You could go over to her apartment with some torches and pitchforks just to show you mean business."

"Lorenzo, you are being ridiculous," Mom said. She liked and respected her principal. She and Greg Maynard were not only colleagues, but also good friends. Sometimes Jaris feared they liked each other too much. Mom was attractive and Maynard was divorced.

"Leave McDowell alone, for crying out loud," Pop persisted. "She's the kid's last chance. She won't step over the line by letting druggies hang out there. She's too smart for that. Just give her some space and she'll be fine. She might even save the kid."

"Pop's right," Jaris agreed. "Ms. McDowell is the smartest teacher at school. She wouldn't do anything that'd cause trouble. Everybody likes her. She makes history fun and exciting. Even kids who hate history like her class."

Mom looked at Jaris, a stern look on her face. "Sweetie," she told him, "it's nice to be compassionate, but you have to be realistic too. Remember a couple of months ago when you were coming home late from work? You saw Shane Burgess tagging with some other gang members. Remember how nervous it made you? Well, do you want Shane and his friends hanging around Tubman?"

"Hey, I got a compromise," Pop offered. "When war is about to break out, the two sides need to compromise. We know the kid is living with his sister. Maybe he's gonna be there for only a week, we don't know. How about if we stay out of it until or unless Ms. McDowell does something that causes a problem. Like say the kid is leaning on the statue of Harriet Tubman at school, smoking weed as everybody is streaming out. And along comes Ms. McDowell and she shouts, 'That's my little bro. He's got more baggies where that came from. Way to go, Sparky.' Then we call out the infantry, okay?"

"As usual, you're being ridiculous, Lorenzo, but you have a point," Mom conceded. "I can live with that. If the profile is very low, so be it. I don't like the idea of a boy like that living with a teacher, but if everything is kept very low-key, okay."

"You hear her, Jaris? You hear your mother?" Pop howled. "The lady is agreeing with me. You hear what I'm saying, boy? She is conceding that her grease monkey man might just have hit on a good compromise. This is a big red-letter day!"

Mom meant to look angry, but she laughed. "Lorenzo," Mom admitted, "there are times when I ask myself why I married you. Aside from being the handsomest boy I knew, you are moody and unreasonable and very difficult to live with, but then you act like you just did and you make me laugh. Underneath all those dark moods there is a delightfully funny man trying to get out."

Jaris was relieved that Ms. McDowell was in no immediate danger of being questioned about her brother. Jaris felt really sorry for her. If she loved Shane half as much as Jaris loved Chelsea, then there was no way she could turn her back on him. Jaris could imagine if Chelsea was in some kind of trouble. Jaris would move heaven and earth to help her. He'd make sure she had a safe refuge no matter what anybody said or did.

After school the next day, Jaris was thinking about trying the new pineapple-topped pizza at the restaurant across the street. It was only a half block from Tubman High School, and Sami and Trevor were already raving about the new pizza.

Jaris saw Sereeta talking to some friends in front of the school, and he waited patiently for the chance to invite her for pizza. Jaris hadn't asked Sereeta out since their movie date. Everything had gone so well that night that he was eager for a second date, even if only for pizza. But it seemed like Sereeta was never alone. She was always in a group of friends.

Alonee came along, holding her binder against her chest. She was wearing a bright red pullover.

"I've never seen you in red before, Alonee," Jaris commented, "you look good."

Alonee smiled. "I saw this sweater on sale and it fit me really good so—"

"I'll say it fits you good," Jaris repeated.

"Say what?" Alonee asked in surprise. A smile crinkled her mouth.

Jaris felt his face grow warm. "Uh, just that the sweater fits you great. Looks real nice, Alonee," he said.

Sereeta was still deep in conversation with her friends. "Hey Alonee, have you tried the pineapple pizza over there yet?" Jaris asked.

"No, have you?" Alonee replied.

"Let's go try it," Jaris suggested. "I got some good tips about it at work, and the tab's on me."

Alonee shrugged. "I never turn down a good pizza," she said, falling in step beside Jaris.

As they crossed the street, it dawned on Jaris that he'd never taken Alonee out. They had never had a date. She was dear to him, but they just never got to dating. Not that this was a date. It was just two friends going for a pizza, and Jaris happened to be paying. But it surprised him to realize they'd never gone to a movie or a concert together in all the time they knew each other.

"This is really good," Alonee remarked, tasting the pineapple pizza. "I thought it'd be good but it's even better than I expected."

"Yeah," Jaris agreed. "They got good pizza here." After a minute or so, Jaris mentioned, "Sami said Maya is really cranky about her crutches, poor kid."

"Yeah," Alonee acknowledged. "You just take it for granted when you've got two good legs that you can go anywhere you want and do stuff without even thinking. And then when something like that happens, it like turns your world upside down."

Jaris couldn't take his eyes off the sweater and how it set off Alonee's cute figure. Alonee noticed Jaris looking at her and she asked, "Do I owe this pizza entirely to my red sweater, Jaris?"

Jaris laughed. "Nah," he answered. "The sweater caught my eye, but I wanted to try the pizza and I knew I'd enjoy it more with you. You know, Alonee, you're special to me. You're one of my best friends."

"Sort of like a really nice sister, huh?" Alonee responded in a faintly forlorn voice.

"I didn't say that," Jaris said.

"No, I know you didn't," Alonee agreed. The look of sadness passed through her eyes. Then she smiled and the sadness seemed to fade. It was like a cloud momentarily over the sun, hurrying off to let the sunlight through again.

Jaris felt strange. He liked Alonee, and he knew she liked him. But now, if only for a moment, he was afraid she liked him in a different way than he liked her.

CHAPTER THREE

Jaris's parents had agreed that one of them would drive him home whenever he worked late at the Chicken Shack. But on Saturday, Jaris got off at two in the afternoon. As he was walking home, he noticed someone falling in step behind him.

"Hey, Jare the Hare, you walk pretty fast," B.J. Brady called out.

"Hey B.J.," Jaris called back. "I'm anxious to get home and start in on my ton of homework. I got book reports and research papers . . . you name it."

"Oh man, I'm glad I'm not at the brain factory anymore," B.J. said. "Knocking yourself out writing and churning out a bunch of paper and for what? For a chump change job in some stuffy office, kowtowing to The Man. Me, I'm free as a bird and living the good life."

Then B.J. changed the subject. "Hey, how about that little sister getting capped the other night in front of the deli? Now that is notcool man."

"Yeah. Maya is doing better but it was an awful thing. The bullet could have hit her artery and killed her. These gangbangers have no consciences," Jaris lamented.

"I beg to differ my man," B.J. objected. "I'm pretty well plugged in on the street. There's no big wars going on right now. I talked to a lot of dudes, and nobody knows anything about the shooting. Here's the thing, Jaris. The gangbangers did not do it."

"They always clam up when something like that goes down B.J. You know they won't rat on each other. Their whole deal is not cooperating with the police. Even the rappers support that," Jaris said.

"I hear you man, but this is different. They talk to me. They know that B.J. Brady is not down with the police. They tell me what's going down, and nobody knows the guys who hit the sister. For one thing, most of the guys like the dude who runs the deli. He gives credit to their families when they're hard up for Sunday dinner. Why would they pull something like this in front of his deli and ruin his business?" B.J. asked.

"All I know is that an innocent little girl has gotten a lot of pain and discomfort that she doesn't deserve," Jaris said.

He took a closer look at B.J. He was a far cry from the wisecracking little ninth grader who had so many friends at Tubman. True, he was flunking all his classes back then, but no kid was more popular. B.J. bragged about having it made now, and he wore good clothes and a lot of gold chains around his neck. His pockets were fat with money. But his eyes carried a deep sadness. The drugs could raise his mood, but they couldn't cure the wounds. "Hey B.J.," Jaris started to say, "I know you cut your ties with your parents when you dropped Tubman, but—"

"They cut me off first," B.J. corrected Jaris. "The deal was 'stay in school and bring those grades up.' No can do, so they showed me the door."

"I was wondering if you ever see them . . . or hear from them or something," Jaris ventured.

"That was the end of it. Done and gone man. Last words I heard from my old man was when he was cussing me out," B.J. said.

"But your mom . . . a mom would want to at least hear from her kid," Jaris said. "A card or a phone call . . . "

"She's dead," B.J. told Jaris. His voice was matter-of-fact. But his chin trembled a little at saying the words.

"When did that happen?" Jaris asked.

"Few weeks ago," B.J. replied. A shadow went through his eyes, like a ghost escaping from hiding.

"Did you get to go to the funeral?" Jaris asked.

"No. I didn't even know she was dead 'til I read the obit in the paper a couple days after she was cremated," B.J. explained.

"Oh man, I'm sorry," Jaris said. "That's rough."

B.J. smiled. It wasn't a regular smile. It was a clown's smile, totally fake and almost painted on. A smile that meant nothing. "No problem," he grinned. "Like they say, it is what it is." Then he added, "See man, the way it ought to be in a family, you know, like they stick with you even though you're no good. They can yell at you and stuff, but they can't toss you out and change the locks on the doors. They do that—it's over. My folks, they just tossed me out like a mop that ain't worth cleaning no more. They were done with me."

Jaris thought of Ms. McDowell and Shane. That's why she was going the extra mile for Shane. She was family. She knew the meaning of family.

When Jaris arrived at school early Monday morning, a group of his friends were talking near the library. Trevor, Sami, Alonee, and DeWayne were in deep conversation. It seemed to Jaris that DeWayne had gotten over being mad at him for bringing up Jacklyn's story. Jaris was glad it was behind him.

"Maya is really upset about all the stuff she can't do anymore," Sami was saying. "She's so frustrated."

"It must be hard," Alonee remarked.

Sami turned and looked at DeWayne then. "Remember last summer when you came back from Florida wearing that cast on your arm? That must have been hard for you, DeWayne. Maybe you should come talk to Maya and help her feel she's not the only person in the world ever had to deal with stuff like this."

"Sure," DeWayne agreed. "Anything I can do to help. I don't know if you guys know it or not, but most summers I spend with my grandparents in Florida. We moved, but they're still there. They love deep-sea fishing. Little town there with nothing going on, but my grandfather and some other guys get in some great fishing."

"Is that how you broke your arm?" Jaris asked. "Hauling in a big fish?"

"Uh . . . no, I wish. Actually there was an auto accident. I was lucky to have just minor injuries," DeWayne said.

"Your grandparents retired?" Alonee asked.

"No, matter of fact my grandfather is the town sheriff. It's a really cool job because there's not much crime in Palmetto Frond Junction," DeWayne answered.

"Hey!" Sami exclaimed. "We got something in common, DeWayne. My uncle is a police officer here in town. And he's got a lot to do. So you and me got kinfolk wearing badges."

DeWayne laughed. "Mostly grandpa makes sure nobody is fishing without a license," he chuckled.

"Palmetto Frond Junction," Trevor commented, "now that's a name for you."

Later that afternoon, Mattie Archer went out to her mailbox and found something strange. A large bouquet of red roses lay at the base of the mailbox post. Attached to the stems of the roses was an envelope, and the name on the envelope was "Maya." But the name wasn't written. It was made of letters cut out of a magazine and pasted together. Mattie yelled for her husband.

"Lonnie! Come see this!" she cried. She was surprised and then frightened.

"What's wrong?" Lonnie Archer asked. He'd just got home from work and was about to get into the shower when he heard his wife yelling. He was wearing a bathrobe.

"Look at this," Mattie said. "Somebody left these roses for our little girl, and this envelope." She took out a note that was wrapped around a hundred dollar bill. The note was written in the same way as Maya's name on the envelope, the letters cut from a magazine.

"Sorry little girl. Sorry you got hurt."

Lonnie stared at the note, frowning in confusion. "Must be somebody read in the newspaper about Maya getting shot. They wanted to do something nice to make her feel better," Lonnie suggested. "But how come the note and Maya's name is made from cutout letters? Seems like this person wants to hide who they are."

"Maybe they just didn't want somebody tracking them down and thanking them—or bein' suspicious," Mattie guessed.

"Wha—?" Lonnie exclaimed. "There's more here. On the back of the note."

"Forgive me," the magazine cutout words said on the other side of the note.

Sami told everybody at school about the red roses, the hundred dollars, and the note. "We thought some stranger just felt bad about Maya gettin' hurt like that and sent the stuff. You know, one of those random acts of kindness kind of things. But then the rest of the note said 'Forgive me,' so it had to be from the shooter."

Derrick Shaw, who usually didn't get things right, made a smart comment. "The shooter is feeling guilty. When gangbangers shoot people, they don't feel guilty. Had to be somebody else who shot Maya, not a gangbanger."

"Yeah," Jaris agreed. "And he covered up his handwriting. He must have shot Maya by mistake. Sami, I hope you told the police about all this."

"Oh yeah. We called my uncle right away, and he and another policeman came to the house. They took the note and the envelope. I guess my parents touched everything, so maybe it won't make such good evidence," Sami said. "We gave them the hundred dollar bill too, but they said they'd give it back. We want to do something nice for Maya with it."

DeWayne Pike had been standing at the edge of the cluster of friends talking about the strange gift. Jaris glanced at him a couple of times. DeWayne looked nervous. He was chewing on his lower lip and blinking really fast. That kind of behavior was unusual for him. When they were rehearsing for the play, even when things were going badly and everyone was tense, DeWayne always kept his cool and calmed everybody down. Now he looked really agitated.

At lunchtime, Jaris and Alonee went over to an isolated bench under the eucalyptus tree. They had privacy there. Jaris knew he could trust Alonee with any information and be sure it would go no further. "Alonee, this is going to sound really crazy. I hope I'm wrong, but I'm pretty sure the guy who shot Maya was aiming at DeWayne Pike," Jaris confided.

Alonee had been eating a grilled cheese sandwich, and now her eyes popped wide open. "*What*?" she exclaimed.

"Well, Jacklyn Webster has been saying all along that DeWayne ducked before the shots were fired, like he spotted something suspicious about the car that slowed down and he felt he was in danger, so he hit the dirt. And today, when we were talking about the guy who sent that gift to Maya, I happened to look at DeWayne, and he seemed really uptight and worried," Jaris went on.

"I heard that about Jacklyn, but I thought she just got mixed up," Alonee commented. "So you think somebody is gunning for DeWayne? He's a good guy. He's never been in a gang. He comes from a good family. I mean, his grandfather is the sheriff in that little town in Florida. Why would anybody want to shoot him?"

"I don't know. I told you it was going to sound crazy, Alonee. But if it's true and the guy hit Maya by mistake, he feels guilty and he's trying to make amends," Jaris explained.

"Well, what should we do?" Alonee asked. "I mean, if some nut is gunning for DeWayne, then we're all in danger being close to him."

"We've got to talk to him, Alonee. He was really defensive when I talked to him before about what Jacklyn saw that night. A bunch of us—you, me, Sami, and Trevor— we got to confront him together and get the truth," Jaris insisted.

After school, Alonee and Jaris approached DeWayne as he came from his drama class. "Hey man, we're all going over for pizza.

We're checking out that new pineapple-topped pizza. Want to come along?"

"Sure," DeWayne agreed. "I haven't tried that yet. I've been wanting to."

The five Tubman High students crossed the street, and Jaris led the way to the most secluded booth. DeWayne started to look nervous. "Something going on here?" he asked.

Sami was appointed to be the one bringing up the subject. Her family had suffered from what had happened that night. "DeWayne, we all your friends. You know that. You helped me so much with my role in the play. But my little sister almost got killed the other night, and our family went through hell. Hear what I'm sayin'?" she began.

"Yeah, but—" DeWayne started to say.

"DeWayne," Sami continued in a stern voice, "you gotta be straight with us. Do you have an enemy out there who might have been shooting at you that night Maya got hit? It's not your fault man. We're not blaming you if some crazy guy is after you, but you need to level with us, and we'll all help. We're friends. We got each other's backs. You don't have to be afraid to tell us the truth."

DeWayne Pike buried his face in his hands for a few seconds. When he faced the other four, he looked stricken. 'You guys . . . I'm sorry. Sami, *I'm so sorry* . . . " His voice was barely a whisper. "There was a guy in Florida . . . my grandfather sent him to prison, and he always claimed he was framed. He blamed Grandpa. When he got out of prison, he had a lot of hate. He tried to get even with my grandfather through me. He tried to run me down with his car once. He was arrested and sent to a mental hospital. We thought he'd never get out. We forgot all about him. Somehow he got out, I guess. He tracked me here. The other night, I saw this car—he always drove a black car with flames painted on the sides. I panicked. I ducked. Then Maya got shot. I'm so sorry . . . it just all happened so fast my reflexes kicked in."

"It's not your fault, DeWayne," Sami said, "but the police have got to be looking for this dude, you hear me? Like right now."

"My parents called the police that night. They got in touch with my grandfather in Florida and got a description of the guy and his car. They've been looking for him since the shooting. But he's like dropped off the radar. I guess he's hiding out," DeWayne explained. "I should have been up front with you guys from the gitgo. I was just so ashamed and sad that something in my past caused your little sister to get hurt, Sami. And, yeah, I was ashamed of ducking. I feel like a coward."

"It's not your fault DeWayne," Sami consoled him, patting him on the shoulder. "I'm just glad we know now what was going down."

When DeWayne left, the four remaining at the table looked at one another.

"That's really awful," Trevor commented. "A guy coming all the way from Florida to shoot a teenaged boy for something his grandfather is supposed to have done."

"Grudges last a long time, I guess," Alonee said.

Jaris was confused. Why didn't DeWayne tell them all this immediately? They were all in danger if a dangerous man was gunning for him. And did they now know the whole story? Jaris wasn't sure. DeWayne had already lied. Maybe the lies were not over.

When Jaris got home, his mother was talking about church. She was a great admirer of the new, young pastor, Eugene Bromley. "Pastor Bromley sees alcohol as the most dangerous drug in our neighborhood," she was saying. "It kills more people in auto accidents than any other drug, and it breaks up more marriages too. So he's forming an antialcohol group in our church for young and old. People are going to make pledges to stop drinking and causing havoc in their families."

Pop was sitting there watching the sports news on television. "It makes me mad when some teams keep winning every season just because they got the money to hire the best players. Doesn't seem fair," Pop growled.

"You didn't hear a word I said, Lorenzo," Mom complained.

"You were saying something about Pastor Bromley," Pop answered her. "How good his sermons are or something."

"Lorenzo, Pastor Bromley wonders why you don't come to church more often," Mom remarked. "He said last Easter you came, and he noticed you had a fine baritone voice that filled the whole church, and it would be nice if you came every Sunday."

"Well," Pop countered, "you tell Pastor Bromley to call on Mister Jackson and to counsel him to stop making me work so hard so I wouldn't be too tired to come to church on Sunday and listen to Pastor Bromley shoot off his mouth about the sinners he's trying to corral."

"Lot of men in our neighborhood have alcohol problems," Mom said. "That's why

Pastor Bromley thinks this antialcohol group where they take the pledge against drinking is a good idea."

"Well that doesn't concern me," Pop protested. "Because I don't have an alcohol problem."

Mom rolled her eyes. She glanced over at Jaris, who was trying to flee the argument by hurrying through the living room and hiding in his bedroom. "Jaris, you be honest now. Have you ever seen your father when he has had too much to drink?" Mom demanded.

Jaris felt miserable. There was no way in the world he was going to embarrass his father. Pop was down on himself most of the time anyway without his own son reminding him of his failings. Still, Pop did have a problem. Sometimes when Pop had a bad day at the garage, he stopped at his favorite bar and had one too many. It usually happened on Friday nights, and the whole family would await his return nervously.

"I think Pastor Bromley is a really smart guy," Jaris responded. "Because like we're always hearing a lot of warnings about drugs, but lots of kids get drunk at parties every weekend and go around driving and hurting people. So it'd be good if everybody kind of just quit drinking." Jaris knew he had not answered Mom's question and she wouldn't be pleased, but it was the best he could do without hurting Pop's feelings.

"Once in a while, maybe, I stop at the Lucky Bar and have one little drink," Pop admitted. "So that's a problem, Monie?"

"Lorenzo, you know it's more than that," Mom insisted.

"I got to be a saint to fit the requirements for being a husband to Monica Spain now," Pop stormed. "The last time I got my driver's license renewed, they gave me this little paper telling how much a man of my weight can drink without breaking the law, and I stick very closely to that. I do not drive unless I am well within the limits on that piece of paper."

"Well," Mom sniffed, "I have my doubts about that. But I don't see why you can't come down to the meeting where the families are going to discuss this pledge and just listen. You could at least do that."

"I don't need no needle-nosed minister carping at me about problems I don't have," Pop growled. "When I'm out there driving, I see men lying around the sidewalk too drunk to know what city they live in. You tell Pastor Bromley to go out and minister to those poor devils. He needs to come out of his ivory tower and rub shoulders with people in the real world."

"Well," Mom said in a hurt voice, "I'll just tell you this. On Friday nights this whole family just holds their breaths waiting for you to come home. And if you're late, our hearts are in our mouths thinking about what might have happened with you driving home in *that condition*."

"*That condition!*" Pop mocked Mom's voice. "Listen to her, Jaris. From the sound of the woman, I come staggering in every

Friday night, and I got a stack of DUIs on the kitchen table, when the truth is I've never got a DUI in my whole life and I never will."

Jaris escaped from the room before Mom could try again to enlist him in the battle to convince Pop he had a problem.

Jaris started work on a research paper he was doing for history. Ms. McDowell wanted everybody to read and note different views on the Vietnam War and reach a conclusion about the American policy at the time.

While Jaris was working, Chelsea came to his door. "Hi Jare, wasup?" she asked.

"Nothing much. Mom's trying to get Pop down to church to that antialcohol meeting Pastor Bromley is setting up. Pastor Bromley is trying to get as many people as possible to pledge to lay off the demon rum," Jaris answered.

Chelsea giggled. "What's the demon rum?" she asked.

"You know, booze," Jaris said.

65

"I like Pastor Bromley," Chelsea replied. "He's so funny. When he takes the kids on field trips and camping, he's like a little kid himself. He's more excited than we are when we see some wild animal. He'll go, 'Oh, there's a red-tailed hawk. Did you see it?' Or, 'Oh, a jackrabbit. A big whopper of a jackrabbit!'" Then Chelsea looked serious and went on, "Maya told me the man who shot her sent her roses and a hundred dollars, and he said he was sorry."

"Yeah," Jaris said. "He didn't mean to shoot her. I guess he's sorry about that."

"Sami told Maya he meant to shoot DeWayne Pike. I don't know why. DeWayne is nice, isn't he? I liked him in the play. Why would somebody want to shoot him, Jaris?" Chelsea wondered.

Jaris put his hands on Chelsea's shoulders and explained, "It's kind of complicated, chili pepper. DeWayne told us that there's a man in Florida who's mad at his grandfather. So the man is trying to hurt DeWayne as a way of getting back at his granddad. DeWayne and his parents told the police all about this man, and they're out catching him right now so he can't hurt anybody else."

Chelsea's eyes grew very big. "You better stay away from DeWayne until the police catch that man. You remember how everybody said in the play that Sydney Carton and Charles Darnay looked alike? You and DeWayne do too. Maybe that man will see you and think you're DeWayne, or else he'll shoot you because you're standing close to DeWayne like Maya was," Chelsea said.

"Not to worry, chili pepper," Jaris assured her with a confidence he did not feel. "I bet they'll catch that guy really quick. Maybe they have him already."

Reassured, Chelsea smiled.

CHAPTER FOUR

When Jaris saw DeWayne at school the next day, he asked him if his family had heard anything about the investigation of the shooter.

"My grandfather is e-mailing all kinds of stuff to the police here," DeWayne explained, "so they know more about the guy and what his patterns of behavior are. Grandpa thinks he might not even be alive anymore. He probably feels so guilty about shooting that little girl that he might have offed himself already. He tried to kill himself once in Florida. He's a real whacko. Be a good thing if he was dead."

Jaris grew more puzzled than ever. What sort of a person was this? He tries to kill an innocent teenager like DeWayne just to even the score with his lawman grandfather? And he feels so guilty about accidentally shooting a child that he sends her roses and money. "DeWayne," Jaris asked, "was this guy a serious criminal when your grandfather arrested him?"

DeWayne got a pained expression on his face. "You know, Jaris, I'd just rather not talk about it. It's a really painful thing. I'd rather just put it behind me and hope the guy jumped in the bay. I hope he's swimming with the fishes right now," DeWayne responded.

"Yeah, I hear what you're saying, DeWayne," Jaris agreed. "Hey, did you hear from the local TV station yet? Some lady from there called me and said they were doing a piece on our play. Actually, it's about that playwright, Jeannie Duvall, who adapted the play from *A Tale of Two Cities* but they want some footage of the kids who were in the play to spice up the story. She's a big thing now. That'd be cool to be on TV, huh?"

"Yeah," DeWayne replied, brightening. "You know, I'm going to major in drama in college. I'm hoping for a career in show business. How about you, Jaris? The acting bug bite you too?"

"Nah," Jaris said. "Playing Sydney Carton was the high point of my career. It was a blast, but I wouldn't want to do it for a living. No way. It's scary getting out there and performing every night. I've been kicking some other ideas around for my future. Don't laugh, but I think I might like to be a teacher. A teacher like Torie McDowell. And, you know, like my mom. My mom teaches fourth grade and she really helps the kids."

"That'd be great," DeWayne remarked. "A good solid career. But not for me. I enjoy taking risks. I like to go flying with no safety net under me. I need the adrenalin rush, you know what I mean?"

"When my mom first started teaching," Jaris went on, "she took over a classroom that was really a mess. The regular teacher had lost all the kids. Mom went in there, a young teacher, got everybody in line and enjoying learning. We were really proud of her."

"Well, teachers do a lot of good," DeWayne said, "but they don't make much money. Not like successful people in show business. I mean, actors can make mega-bucks. I'd like really to make it big, Jaris."

"Well, good luck man," Jaris told him.

When Jaris went home that day, it dawned on him that he had kept his pride in his mother's classroom achievements pretty much to himself. She was really good at what she did, and Jaris now thought that it wouldn't hurt him to let her know he thought she was a great teacher.

Jaris spent all his energy in trying to build up his father. Dad was always regretting not having accomplished more in life, and Jaris thought he needed encouragement. But in his zeal to build up Pop, Jaris knew he had taken his mother for granted.

When Jaris came in the house, Mom was finishing some work on the computer.

She looked up and smiled. "How's every-thing, sweetie?" she asked.

"Okay, Mom. DeWayne and his grandfather are telling the police all about this weird guy who shot at him at the deli. DeWayne thinks they'll get the guy fast, or else maybe he feels so guilty about shooting a little girl that he'll kill himself before the police get him. DeWayne is hoping for that. Then it'd be over," Jaris related.

Mom shook her head. She knew all about Maya getting red roses and a hundred dollars probably from the shooter. Jaris had told her everything DeWayne had to say about the matter. "You know, Jaris," Mom started saying, "I wouldn't want to hope any man commits suicide. The man needs our prayers. He must be horribly mixed up in his mind to go gunning for a young man just to avenge something the grandfather supposedly did to him. He almost killed a beautiful young girl but he does feel remorse. That means there is something good in him. That means he might repent."

Pastor Bromley was always talking about repentance. Nobody is too bad to repent, he often said in his sermons. Forgiveness is there for the worst sinners if only they ask for it. Jaris's mother really took that to heart, but Jaris found it harder to do that. He couldn't imagine how the shooter could justify trying to kill DeWayne over something DeWayne had nothing to do with.

Mom went on, "It would be tragic if the terrible events were compounded by the man taking his own life. No matter how awful our lives have been, there is always hope."

"Hey Mom," Jaris said, "me and DeWayne were sorta talking about what we wanted to do when high school was over. DeWayne wants to be an actor, get into show business, and make a ton of money. Well, I have this pretty good voice. People tell me that anyway. And I thought I could maybe use that in my own career."

"Do you want to be an actor too?" Mom asked in surprise.

"No way!" Jaris exclaimed, "Sydney Carton was my first and last acting role. But I'm kinda kicking an idea around right now. I think maybe I finally know what I'll go for in college."

Mom beamed. She gave Jaris her full attention. She liked nothing better than for her children to share their dreams with her. They didn't do so too often. "Tell me, sweetheart," she encouraged him. "I can't wait!"

"Well, I think maybe I'll try to be a teacher Mom," Jaris announced.

For a moment Mom looked stunned. Then she smiled and cried, "A teacher!"

"Yeah Mom. You're so good at it. I thought maybe I got some of your teaching genes," Jaris explained.

"Oh Jaris!" Mom jumped up, ran to Jaris, and gave him a big hug. Mom was small, but she hugged him with such force that it took his breath away. "You've made me so happy and it's not even my birthday or Mother's Day!"

"Yeah well, I'm kinda thinking about it," Jaris said. "A lot of the kids in my class are thinking about college and stuff, and what they want to do. We'll be seniors next year. Sami was thinking maybe she wanted to study business, but when Maya got hurt and she saw how great the physical therapists were working with her, now Sami thinks she might want to be a physical therapist."

"That's wonderful Jaris. Sami is a good-hearted girl, and she'd be very capable at that," Mom said.

Pop's green pickup pulled into the driveway just then and he came in. "What a day," he grumbled. "They all own junkers these days. Nobody has got the money to buy a decent car. So they run these beaters into the ground, and every once in a while I'm supposed to work miracles with them. Those cars should be crushed in the junkyard, but, no, I gotta revive them."

Jaris thought briefly about what his father, Lorenzo, had told him so often.

When his pop was sixteen years old, he had his dreams too. He was going to study science in college. He was going to work in a lab and make important discoveries. But none of it happened. Now Jaris had mixed feelings about sharing his own dreams with his father, but he decided to do it anyway.

"You know what Pop?" he declared, "I'm thinking maybe of being a teacher, you know, going for that in college."

Pop stood there for a moment with no expression on his face. Then he said, "Good solid choice, boy. I married a teacher, you know, and for all her bossiness and ornery ways, I've never regretted it. I would go over there right now and give that prissy lady a big hug and a kiss, but I got motor oil from a Toyota, brake fluid from a Camaro, and unknown grease stains from half a dozen other beaters on my hands and face."

Mom laughed. Jaris was glad to hear her laugh at Pop's jokes. Jaris hated it when his parents argued—and they argued too often—but right now, things were good and Jaris relished the feeling.

Jaris had been working up the courage to ask Sereeta for another date, but the shooting at the deli delayed him. Everybody was so upset that asking for a date seemed stupid. But now that DeWayne seemed so confident that the shooter would be caught soon, Jaris thought about going out with Sereeta again.

On Friday, Jaris saw Sereeta sitting by herself, eating lunch under the eucalyptus tree. Usually she was surrounded by friends and Jaris lost his nerve. But now conditions looked perfect. Jaris clutched his salami sandwich and walked over to where she was sitting.

"Some company okay, Sereeta?" Jaris asked her. He was nervous. He was surprised at how nervous he was.

Sereeta looked up and said, "Sure."

"You eat already?" Jaris remarked, noticing that she had no empty lunch bag or anything.

"I wasn't hungry today," Sereeta replied.

"Uh, how's everything going?" Jaris asked her.

"Mom is about a month away from having the baby," Sereeta explained. "She and my stepfather have filled the nursery with all kinds of stuff. I never realized they made so many things for babies. I mean, hanging mobiles, musical mobiles. Everything is blue. Even the walls are painted blue. I guess that's good because blue is a good color for me right now."

"They found out it's a boy, huh?" Jaris asked.

"Oh yes. My stepfather wanted a son. He's got little toy footballs, basketballs, baseballs all over the place," Sereeta answered. She had a thin smile on her lips, as if she were talking about somebody else's family, not hers.

Sereeta was talking as if she was not connected to this new family, to her stepfather or even to her mother. She seemed as if, when the baby boy arrived, she would even be less connected.

"Well, a baby is a lot of work," Jaris commented. "It's not all fun and games."

"I hope the baby is an absolute monster," Sereeta said in a burst of bitterness that even changed the features of her face. She looked hard and almost evil. "I hope he barfs all over her dresses. I hope he yells all night and they don't get a minute's sleep. I know that's terrible of me. I feel so bad to be talking like this. I hate myself for the feelings I have."

Jaris felt sorry for Sereeta. When her parents divorced, she was in middle school, and the divorce tore her apart. Then, when both her parents remarried, it was another trauma for her. Sereeta felt lost in the shuffle. Her world was changing. It was peopled now with strangers. She couldn't recognize her place anymore. Sometimes she thought her place did not exist at all.

Sereeta reached down into the grass and plucked a wide blade. She began slowly stripping it into threads with her fingernails. She was looking down, staring at the blade of grass as if it were really important. Then she said in a voice that was barely audible, "They never saw the play."

"What?" Jaris exclaimed. Then he knew. In *A Tale of Two Cities*, Sereeta had the major female role as Lucie. She was excellent. "They didn't see it?"

"No. They never saw me playing Lucie," Sereeta sighed. "I don't think they even *knew* I was playing Lucie. They knew I was in the play though. I told them. Each night I'd look out over the audience and I'd expect to see them, but I didn't ever see them. They said they would come for the last performance, but then something came up and they couldn't."

Jaris didn't know what to say. His own parents came for every performance, just to watch him play Sydney Carton. Grandma Jessie came to two performances. Sami's parents came, and even the parents of the bit players came. They would sit there beaming at their children who came on stage to say perhaps four lines.

Jaris had not realized until now that Sereeta's mother and her stepfather did not come at all. His heart ached for her, but he didn't know what to say to make her feel better.

"He . . . my stepfather . . . wanted to see the Dodger game . . . my mother, she, uh . . . never cared for baseball but now she's a sports freak for him. He wanted to see the Dodger game that last . . . night . . . so . . . they didn't come."

Suddenly Sereeta was crying, not normally, with soft sobs, but wildly and convulsively weeping. Tears ran down her face and she was shaking violently.

Jaris wanted to take Sereeta in his arms and comfort her. But when he knelt down in the grass beside her and touched her shoulder, she pulled away and whispered, "Go away—please go away . . . just go away."

"Sereeta, there's gotta be something I can do for you," Jaris pleaded.

"Will you please go away!" she cried. She lay down in the grass, her face turned toward the weathered bark of the eucalyptus tree, her face away from Jaris. She shook with sobs and then she was still. "I wish I was dead," she murmured.

"Sereeta no, don't say that," Jaris begged. "Please don't say that. Listen, I'll take you somewhere right now, anywhere."

Slowly she sat up. "I've got biology," she said in a voice hoarse from crying.

"You don't have to go to biology," Jaris urged. "We'll go somewhere right now."

Sereeta gathered her books and her binder. "I'll go to biology," she declared.

"Then after biology we'll meet right here, okay?" Jaris said. "Right after the last bell, I'll meet you here, okay? And we'll go someplace, anyplace you say."

"Okay," she agreed. She dried her eyes with the back of her hand. "I look terrible, don't I?"

"No, you look fine," Jaris replied. "Don't forget, we'll meet right here."

"Okay," she said again. Then she got up and ran toward biology because the bell was due to ring any minute.

Jaris felt drained. He couldn't understand how Sereeta's mother was acting. Couldn't she see what was happening to her daughter? Was she so wrapped up in her new husband and the coming baby that she was blind to what was going on with Sereeta? Didn't she see the pain? Didn't she realize that Sereeta was feeling more and more abandoned, like she didn't matter at all anymore?

Jaris felt himself hating Sereeta's parents. He didn't even really know them, but he hated them, all four of them. Sereeta's mother and father and the stepparents. They were all failing her.

How could they all be so selfish?

Jaris sat through his science class counting the minutes when he could meet Sereeta and take her somewhere so she could forget her problems for a little while.

Mr. Buckingham was, as usual, denouncing the forces that were damaging the environment. He glared out at his students and cried, "When these despoilers have totally destroyed the earth, I shall be dead. But you, the young, you will suffer the consequences, so you should be even more outraged than I am." All Jaris could do was think about Sereeta. When the final bell rang, he planned to escape the classroom and race to the eucalyptus tree where she agreed to be. He would take her somewhere, anywhere, wherever she wanted to go. Jaris would call Mom and explain that he had something really important to do and that he'd be home as soon as he could. Mom would understand. She'd have to understand. Sereeta needed to be with someone right now who cared deeply for her.

When the bell finally rang, Jaris bolted from the room, almost knocking his chair over. He sprinted across the campus toward the eucalyptus tree. But even when he was some distance away, he could that Sereeta she wasn't there. There was nobody on the little knoll. Jaris looked around desperately. Then he went over to the biology classroom. Perhaps Mr. Goodman held the class a few minutes overtime.

Jaris looked into the empty classroom and saw Mr. Goodman sitting at his desk. "Mr. Goodman," Jaris asked breathlessly, "was Sereeta Prince in class today?"

"Yes," he said dryly, looking annoyed.

"I was supposed to meet her after class and she wasn't there," Jaris explained.

"Well, I'm afraid I can't help you there," the teacher responded, returning to his task of correcting papers.

Because she lived farther from Tubman High than most of the students, Sereeta usually took the bus home. There was no school bus, but the local bus picked up some students every day and took them to bus stops near their homes.

Jaris ran to the bus stop where Sereeta often waited. The regulars were there, and Jaris knew a few of them. The bus had not come yet and Sereeta was not there. The bus pulled up then and took everybody away, and Jaris stood there for a few minutes staring at it.

Jaris fumbled for his phone. All the cast members of *A Tale of Two Cities* exchanged cell phone numbers in case something came up about the production. Jaris found Sereeta's number and punched in the numbers.

"Don't transfer me to messages," Jaris pleaded with nobody in particular. He wanted to hear Sereeta's voice and be assured she was all right. He didn't want that creepy little dial tone and its invitation to leave a message. The phone rang several times before Sereeta said, "Hi."

"Sereeta," Jaris asked. "Are you okay? I was so worried about you not being by the tree where we planned to meet."

"Yeah, I'm sorry I didn't meet you, Jaris. I walked over to my grandmother's house. She lives in the apartments on Mohegan Street. She's my father's mom. I told you about her once, I think. She's nice. I called her and I said I was really freaking out about everything, and she said to come over and hang out over the weekend," Sereeta explained. Once she had told Jaris and Alonee that her grandmother was the only one of her relatives whom she still loved.

"You sure you're okay?" Jaris asked.

"Yeah, my granny is making me biscuits with gravy and fried chicken and all the stuff that's not good for me. I feel like a little girl again when everything was . . . you know . . . okay," Sereeta said. "Jaris, thanks for caring about me. I'll see you at school on Monday. I'm, uh, sorry I freaked on you."

Jaris thought it was probably good that Sereeta was with her grandmother. Sereeta was the only child of her father's first marriage and the only grandchild. The grandmother doted on Sereeta, and that's what Sereeta needed right now. Someone she was still special to.

Jaris was usually home by this time. In his anxiety looking for Sereeta, he had not

called home to say he'd be late. Most of the
students were now gone from Tubman,
and the campus was pretty much deserted.
Jaris slung on his backpack and started for
home. As he walked down the sidewalk, an
old car cruised slowly alongside him. Jaris
glanced at the driver. He looked middle-
aged and wore a baseball cap. He looked
confused. Jaris had never seen the car in the
neighborhood before. It was really old, an
ancient Studebaker. They hadn't made cars
like that in ages. The car was painted green,
an ugly house paint green because probably
the guy was too poor to get a real paint job
on his rusty beater.

Jaris went to the side window, which
was open, and asked, "You lost, mister?"

"No . . . I got chest pains. You drive?"
he asked.

"Yeah . . . but look, if you're having a
heart attack I'll get 9-1-1 for you on my
cell," Jaris offered.

"No, it's angina . . . my doctor is at the
urgent care place down the street. He'll

give me pills. If you'd just drive me . . ." the man said.

Jaris came around to the driver's side and, as the man moved over, slid under the wheel. Jaris started the car, and, as the car moved from the curb, he felt a hard object jammed against his side.

"Keep drivin', punk," the man hissed. "I tried to take you out the other night, but this is better. That woulda been too easy, too quick."

Jaris broke into a cold sweat. "Hey what's going on, mister? I don't even know you," he protested.

"Keep driving. I want this to happen out there in the country in a place that's like where you killed her. I want you rollin' dead on the asphalt like she was," the man snarled.

"What are you talking about?" Jaris gasped.

"My daughter. You killed my daughter, punk. What? Have you forgotten her already? You killed her in July, not even a year ago. Did she mean so little to you that you've forgotten her already, you piece of garbage?" the man asked bitterly.

"Wait a minute," Jaris said. "You got it all wrong mister. I never killed anybody. I don't know what you're talking about."

"Pull over under the trees ahead," the man ordered. Then he said, "Look at me Pike, and tell me you don't know what I'm talking about."

They looked alike—DeWayne and Jaris. Everybody said that. That was why the casting for *A Tale of Two Cities* seemed so perfect. Sydney Carton, Jaris's role, and Charles Darney, played by DeWayne, were supposed to look alike for the play to work.

Jaris turned and stared at the man. "I'm not DeWayne Pike. We look a lot alike, but I'm Jaris Spain. We both go to Tubman High. I know him. I know a guy from Florida has been stalking him . . . he said the guy drove a black car with flames painted on the side. I guess you've painted your car recently."

"*Damn!*" the man almost sobbed. "*Damn! Oh nooo.*" His face sank in disappointment. But he still held the gun at Jaris's side and his hand was trembling. Jaris thought he might shoot reflexively. Jaris would be just as dead as if the shot had been on purpose. Jaris realized he was in grave danger from an obviously disturbed man. "He . . . he killed my little girl," he stammered. "She was the only child me and my wife had. Steffi was our whole life. Steffi this and Steffi that. It's all we thought about, talked about. She was going with a young fella . . . maybe getting married. Grandkids. It was our whole life he took."

The gun was not pressed against Jaris's side anymore, but the man still held it. His voice went on, wounded, despairing. "My wife, she never got over it. She tried to throw herself into the casket on top of Steffi. She was never the same. Her heart stopped just a few months later. Doc said it was hardening of the arteries, but it wasn't that. It was a broken heart."

"I'm sorry, mister. I really am," Jaris sympathized.

"So," the man said slowly, "you go to school with Pike. You know him . . . "

"Yeah," Jaris said.

"Did he tell you what happened? Did he tell you why I tried to shoot him at the deli?" the man asked.

"Uh . . . he just said this guy from Florida was after him because the guy had it in for his grandfather. I guess DeWayne's grandfather is the sheriff down there. He said the grandfather arrested you and you were mad, so you wanted to get even with his grandfather by offing DeWayne," Jaris explained.

"Liar!" the man hissed. "It's all lies. He killed my Steffi. She was driving in her little Volkswagen down the road in the evening, coming from school. Here comes this pickup driven by DeWayne Pike. He's drunk as a skunk. He's coming at eighty miles an hour. He runs through the stop sign. There was a stop sign there, but he runs right through it. He T-bones my Steffi's little car. She's all buckled in like she should be. Steffi never took chances. But the little car was crushed. They had to cut the top off to get her out. Oh . . . she didn't look like Steffi anymore . . . I couldn't even let the wife see her. She was only seventeen. She was a baby. She hadn't even lived yet."

"I'm really sorry," Jaris said. "Did they arrest DeWayne for driving under the influence and causing a death? I mean, that's serious stuff."

"So you'd think," the man went on, "but there was a big coverup. Pike, he was okay except he had a broken arm. They took him right to the hospital. The law, they never gave him a test to see about alcohol in his blood. His grandfather took care of that. At the hospital they checked his blood, but then they lost the results. Nice, huh?"

"That's awful," Jaris said.

"Yeah. There were witnesses from the party Pike was at. They said he was so drunk he almost had to crawl to get to his car. The law, they wouldn't talk to the witnesses. They said Pike told them those guys were lying about him. So Pike got away with getting drunk and getting behind the wheel of the pickup and killing my little Steffi," the man said. He finally put the gun in his pocket.

"Now you want to get justice for your daughter with a gun, huh? Mister, it won't work," Jaris said softly.

"I'm taking him out for what he did. I got nothing left to live for. My little girl is gone. My wife is gone. There's no future. It's just a black hole in front of my eyes, a black hole he made," the man sighed.

"Look, you already shot that little girl by mistake. You could have killed her. You almost killed me just now. You've got to get justice in another way. File a lawsuit against Pike in the civil court. You can bring those witnesses in. They'll be heard. At least Pike will have to pay something for what he did."

"That's all hocus-pocus, kid," the man protested. "The deck is stacked against people like me and Steffi. We were poor vegetable farmers down there in Florida. The Pikes got money and power. Nobody's going to listen to a broken-down farmer like me. No, if there's going to be justice, I've got to do it myself. I can't do nothing no more for my Steffi. I can't even buy her a pretty dress for the prom. Boy, she was looking forward to that. But she never got to go. He took it all away. . . . Okay kid. We didn't drive too far. You can hike home. Grab your backpack and get out of here, okay? And when you see Pike at school, tell him to get ready for payback time."

Jaris snatched up his backpack and jumped from the car. Within seconds, the old Studebaker roared away. Only then did he notice the Florida plates on the car.

Jaris stood there in the darkness, shaking. He didn't know what to think. Was the guy who just kidnapped him a complete psycho? Did he actually lose a daughter? Did DeWayne drive drunk and kill his daughter? Did Steffi even exist, or was she a figment of a sick man's imagination? Or was it all the truth and was DeWayne's story a lie?

Jaris used his cell phone to call home. He was glad when Pop answered. "Hey Pop, I'm at that little park about a mile from Tubman. Can you come get me?" Jaris asked.

"You okay?" Pop demanded.

"Yeah, I'm okay," Jaris replied.

Pop arrived quickly. After Jaris got in the truck, he told his father everything. Pop said, "Boy, that was beyond stupid to get in a stranger's car. You could be dead right now. It gives me the chills to think a guy had a gun on you."

"You're right, Pop. He said he was having a heart attack or something. I know it was stupid." Jaris noticed they weren't heading home.

"Where we going Pop?" he asked.

"The police station. You've been kidnapped and threatened. The cops need to get this guy. Even if his story is true, he needs to be stopped before he kills some-body," Pop asserted.

Jaris told the police the whole story, and then he and his father went home.

"You want to tell Mom the story or should I?" Pop asked as they neared home.

"I will," Jaris said, dreading Mom's reaction.

After Jaris told the story, first Mom hugged him, then she cried, and then she screamed. "Don't you *ever* get into a strange car again like that! Oh my Lord! You could have been killed!"

When he got to his room, Jaris called DeWayne. "Hey man, something really awful just happened to me. This weird guy told me he was having a heart attack and would I drive him to the clinic. Like an idiot I got in. He almost shot me thinking I was you. Turns out he's the guy stalking you man."

"Oh man, oh man," DeWayne groaned. "I'm sorry . . . I'm really sorry. You told the cops, right? They should be tracking him right now."

"Yeah, I guess so," Jaris went on. "DeWayne, he told me a whole different story than the one you told me. He said you killed his daughter in an auto accident. He said you were drunk and your grandfather got you off the hook."

DeWayne did not seem shocked. "He's a paranoid psycho. He's got a different story for every day of the week. He's delusional. I hope the cops get him tonight. The trail has to be pretty hot." That was all DeWayne had to say.

When they ended the call, Jaris suddenly felt so tired he sank into bed. He was drained. He didn't know what to believe anymore. He realized that today could have been the last day of his life. It could have happened that quickly, that senselessly.

Jaris thought about Steffi—if there was a Steffi. He thought about a young girl, the daughter of a vegetable farmer, coming home like Jaris just was. She never made it. Her parents were destroyed. Jaris remembered the fear and horror on his father's face at the thought that Jaris had been in danger. He remembered the tears running down Mom's face as she hugged him and how she screamed at him.

Could the man have been lying about it all? His story seemed so heartfelt, so real.

Over the weekend, there was no news of the man who kidnapped Jaris being caught. Apparently he had slipped out of sight again. But he would be back. Jaris had no doubt of that.

CHAPTER FIVE

On Monday Mr. Wingate wanted all the cast of *A Tale of Two Cities* to gather in the auditorium after school. Television reporters and cameras would be there. They were doing background for the story on Jeannie Duvall.

"I guess she's getting to be really important," Alonee commented, "a young black playwright making a name for herself adapting books and writing original plays. They're comparing her to Lorraine Hansberry, that lady who wrote *A Raisin in the Sun* years ago."

"Well, it'll be fun being on TV," Jaris said, but he was still worrying about Sereeta. He had not seen her yet, and he knew if he didn't see her in American history, then something was really wrong. As he walked into the history class, Sereeta was coming in too.

"Mr. Wingate wants us for that TV thing in the auditorium after school," Jaris told her.

"Yeah, I got his e-mail," Sereeta said.

"Everything okay, Sereeta?" Jaris asked anxiously.

"Uh-huh. Granny was good for me," Sereeta replied. "We went to the bay and watched the seagulls. We talked. We talked a lot. Granny is a great talker and listener. I dumped a lot of stuff on her and she listened. It was good."

Jaris wondered if DeWayne Pike would come to the auditorium after school. He had to be concerned knowing that his stalker was in the area. Maybe he didn't want to appear on television when the man might be watching. But when the cast gathered, DeWayne was there, apparently in a good mood.

"Heard anything from the police about that guy, DeWayne?" Jaris asked.

"No. They got to be closing in on him. He's probably scared. When he surfaces again, they'll get him," DeWayne asserted.

Debi Livingstone, one of the local TV reporters, informally interviewed the Tubman actors. As cameras took aim, she smiled at Jaris and said, "I understand you were the hit of the play, and you didn't even have any acting experience. Has the acting bug bitten you now?"

"No," Jaris said through a suddenly dry mouth. "I think I'll be a teacher."

"Good for you!" Livingstone exclaimed, beaming and turning to other cast members. Mr. Wingate looked very pleased when the television crew left.

"You were all very good," he told the students. "I am proud of you."

Jaris had not told any of his friends what his kidnapper had told him about his daughter. Jaris did not want to spread rumors about something that may not be true. The man had leveled serious charges against DeWayne, and Jaris didn't feel right sharing the details with anyone.

But the story of Steffi stuck in Jaris's mind, and when he got home from school he went on the Internet. Supposedly the fatal accident happened in July of last year in the small Florida town of Palmetto Frond Junction. Jaris figured not much happened there, and he might find some news stories about the accident if he put the town in a search engine.

Jaris typed in the town's name and started getting results. The first stories were about large fish caught in the area. Then there were stories about a new hotel being built. But then Jaris found a news item about the death of Stephanie Wilcox. She was killed in a traffic accident on July 5.

Jaris felt all feeling leave his legs. He was numb. So there was a Steffi. Jaris read the brief article.

On Friday night Stephanie Wilcox, seventeen, died in a two-car accident at Sports Line Highway. Her Volkswagen was struck by a pickup truck registered to the Pike family of Palmetto Frond Junction. No one was cited in the accident, which is still under investigation. Pike was treated for moderate injuries and released from a local hospital.

Jaris grew more tense. It seemed the man's story was becoming more credible. Jaris read a second article.

TEEN'S FATHER CHARGES OTHER DRIVER DRUNK

Walter Wilcox, father of Stephanie Wilcox who died in a recent auto accident, is charging that the other driver, a minor, was under the influence of alcohol at the time of the collision. Sheriff Harold Pike said no evidence was uncovered to substantiate these charges.

A third article came into view and Jaris read it.

DISTRAUGHT FATHER OF DEAD TEEN ARRESTED

Walter Wilcox was taken into custody Tuesday morning when he shoved his way into Sheriff Harold Pike's office demanding to see the results of the blood alcohol test for the driver, who is a minor. Pike was involved in the auto accident that killed Wilcox's daughter this month. Wilcox was held for several hours and then released. Sheriff Pike expressed sympathy for the man but said that the records of DeWayne Pike's blood tests have been misplaced by the hospital. Sheriff Pike promised to try to locate them.

Jaris then found the final article relating to the incident.

MAN RESCUED AFTER SUICIDE ATTEMPT IN BAYOU

Walter Wilcox was pulled from Acacia Bayou after attempting to take his own life by jumping off a bridge crossing the bayou. Wilcox recently lost his daughter in an auto accident and his wife from heart problems. He has been hospitalized and mental tests are underway.

All the other local articles dealt with fishing and tourist issues. Jaris leaned back in his chair, saddened and disgusted by what he had learned. DeWayne had initially lied about ducking before the shots were fired at the deli. Then he lied about the man's story about an auto accident. DeWayne knew a dangerous man was stalking him, and, to save his own reputation, he did not share that information with his friends who were endangered too.

Jaris went into the living room, where his father was watching a basketball game. "Pop, I need to talk to you about something," Jaris announced.

"Okay," Pop replied. "The game stinks anyway. These guys can't make a free throw to save their lives." He shut off the

TV and turned toward Jaris. Mom was over at her mother's with Chelsea tonight, and so it was just Jaris and his father. Jaris sat down on the sofa beside his father and told him everything, including what he had learned on the Internet. Pop listened in grim silence to the whole thing.

"Man!" he gasped finally. "So the kid has lied about everything!"

"What do I do, Pop? The whole thing is rotten. I believe the whole story Walter Wilcox told me now. DeWayne's grandfather is the sheriff in that town, and he helped cover for DeWayne. They even got the local hospital to lose the results of his blood alcohol level. Nobody paid for that girl's death. Sure, Wilcox has gone off the deep end. He almost killed Maya, but look what happened to him. He lost his child to a drunk driver who got away with it. Then he lost his wife. He lost everything. DeWayne got away with . . . " Jaris couldn't quite say the word, but his father did.

"Murder," Pop finished the sentence. "That's what he got away with. That's what they call it now when you drive drunk and kill somebody."

"So what do I do, Pop?" Jaris turned to his father.

"You could blow DeWayne's cover and spread it all over Tubman what he did. You could ruin the guy's life, Jaris, and he deserves it. But that wouldn't get him charged with driving drunk. And then there's *this*: Is there a ghost of a chance he wasn't drunk? There's no evidence," Pop offered.

"Yeah, the sheriff saw to that," Jaris agreed. "But the Wilcox guy said he had witnesses to DeWayne getting in that pickup that night too drunk to stand up straight. I told Wilcox to sue in civil court . . ."

"That was good advice," Pop affirmed.

"But the man is so off the wall now," Jaris went on, sadly, "that he doesn't believe in any kind of justice being possible. He thinks the only justice for his daughter will come with his gun."

Just then the phone rang. Jaris picked it up. It was DeWayne Pike, breathing so hard he could hardly speak. "Jaris, turn on the TV man!" he yelled. Then he hung up.

Jaris turned the television back on. The basketball game had been preempted by a local news story. There had been a police chase near Tubman High School. The TV screen glowed with red lights and chopper searchlights. A news reporter announced, "To summarize what has just happened, the police chase ended two blocks from Tubman Senior High School. The man wanted in the shooting of a girl at a deli last month and in the kidnapping of a Tubman junior just this week was cornered by the police. He ran into a light standard and came out of his car with a weapon, according to the police spokesperson. When he refused to drop the gun, he was shot multiple times. We do not know his condition, but he is lying on the ground. He does not seem to be moving."

Jaris stared at the TV screen. His mouth was dry. His chest ached. He felt a sadness he couldn't explain. Walter Wilcox was not a good man. He was dangerous. Maybe at one time in his life he had been a good man. Maybe even for most of his life he had worked hard and loved his family and done no great wrongs. But the daughter he loved was taken from him, and his wife was taken, and the man he blamed for all of his sorrow was never held accountable. The man had nothing left, and into the void came hatred. Now he lay on the ground and he wasn't moving.

The news reporter said in a somber voice, "We are seeing the coroner arrive now. There has been no official word of the death of the man involved in the police chase, but the coroner is coming on the scene . . ."

The phone rang again. It was DeWayne. He was screaming with elation. "Jare, they got him! He's dead. We don't have to worry about him anymore. He's dead, Jare!"

Jaris banged the phone down. When it rang again, he didn't answer it. Jaris walked over to the couch and sat beside his father. DeWayne had yelled so loudly on the phone that Pop had overheard what he said.

Pop reached over and put his arm around Jaris's shoulders, pulling him close. "I know what you're feeling boy. They took everything that poor little man had—his child, his wife, and now his life too. But there was no other way. He could have killed Maya. He might have killed you. Then I'd be like Wilcox. If I lost you or Chelsea, or Monie, I'd be a madman too. That's all that divides the most of us from the guys who lose it—that we haven't been tested. They had to take him down like you would a rabid dog. That's what he had become. Maybe he wanted to die Jaris. Maybe he figured out that was best for him. That's why he came out of that car with the gun in his hand."

Jaris nodded. "Yeah," he murmured.

"Jaris, I'm no Bible thumper like your mother," Pop admitted, "but I pray to

God to have mercy on that man's soul, and I know he'll get more justice and compassion over there than he got on this earth."

Jaris hung his head. "Pop," he said to his father, "how am I going to look at that guy—at DeWayne now? It all seems so meaningless. That girl Steffi dying. Her mother. Wilcox. Poor little Maya getting her leg shattered. It all seems so useless, like life is some stupid crapshoot and nothing good comes out of anything."

Pop reached over and grabbed Jaris's arm. "Listen to me, boy, and listen good. You know your mother has been nagging at me to go down to church and take that no-booze pledge with Pastor Bromley. He's getting all the dudes—young and old—signing up because drunk driving is a big problem, not just around here but all over. At first, I know I told your Mom she's nuts. I don't have a problem with alcohol. But sometimes on Friday nights you and Mom and little Chelsea have stood at that window wondering how old Pop is doing.

And sometimes the old green truck is weaving a little . . . am I right?"

"Yeah, I guess," Jaris admitted.

"Well, this Sunday afternoon when Pastor Bromley puts out the call, I'll be there," Pop said. "I'll stand up there and swear off booze Jaris. It's no good for my liver anyway, but that's not why I'm doing it. I'm doing it for little Maya and for Steffi and her mother and her father. They all suffered because of the drinking DeWayne did. I'm going to make something good come of it. It's *not* going to be meaningless, like you said boy. It is going to mean something. That's what I'm going to do, and I'll stand right up there and say I'm doing this for Monie, and Chelsea and Jaris, my family, and for Maya and especially for little Steffi and her pop."

Jaris leaned over and hugged his father. Jaris didn't cry much, but right now his eyes were wet. His tears ran onto Pop's shoulder.

"This old grease monkey is going to make lemonade out of lemons, Jaris," Pop said. "You hear what I'm saying?"

Just then Mom and Chelsea came home from their visit with Grandma Jessie. Mom stopped and stared at her husband and son. "What's going on?" she demanded.

"Tell Pastor Bromley I'm coming this Sunday, woman," Pop declared. "Your nagging finally paid off. I'm coming to take the pledge! Hallelujah!"

CHAPTER SIX

Jaris had just arrived on the campus of Tubman High when DeWayne Pike approached him. "Hey man, I think we got disconnected on the phone last night," DeWayne said.

"No, I hung up on you," Jaris replied.

No other students were around. It was just Jaris and DeWayne. "What's going on?" DeWayne asked.

"I know about Steffi," Jaris snapped. "I googled it and got the whole story."

DeWayne looked stunned for a moment, then he admitted, "Okay, I lied—"

"You've been lying from the beginning man," Jaris snarled. "One lie after another, after another. Jacklyn said she saw you duck. Oh, wait, yeah, you did duck. Then the lie about your grandfather framing somebody. What's the new lie, DeWayne? I can hardly wait to hear it."

"Okay, I didn't want to talk about the accident. It was a terrible thing. It still haunts me. I feel terrible that the girl got killed. I'd do anything in the world to make that night go away. But I wasn't drunk. Wilcox was wrong," DeWayne insisted. "I was at this party and everybody was drinking, and I told those guys we had to drive home and to knock it off, so they got mad. I just left. But when they heard about the accident they lied about me to get even for razzing them. They said I was drunk too. Wilcox believed their lies. He was so torn up from losing his daughter that he had to blame somebody."

"You know what man?" Jaris said. "There's an old saying, I think the Chinese started it. 'Fool me once, shame on you. Fool me twice, shame on me.' Well, I don't buy what you're telling me right now, okay? It said in one of those news articles about the accident that your blood samples were misplaced so they couldn't prove if you were drunk or not . . . that stinks of a coverup in my book."

"Okay," DeWayne snapped back. "So spread your gossip all over the school man. Have a good time ruining my name and turning everybody against me. If that'll make you happy, then go for it. But I'm innocent. I wasn't drunk that night when my pickup hit the girl's car. She's the one who ran the signal, not me. That's the truth. It was a horrible accident. I'll never forget seeing them cutting her body out of the car. It was awful. I thought, 'Because of me, she's dead.' But I couldn't help it. I never meant for it to happen."

Jaris shook his head. "The girl is dead. Her parents are dead. God knows what you were doing that night and only you know. I don't know for sure. As far as I'm concerned, it's over. That's the end of it. I know what I think, but that's just me," Jaris said.

DeWayne held out his hand. "Thanks man," he offered.

Jaris turned away. "I can't shake your hand. I just can't," he said.

"Your call," DeWayne replied.

Jaris walked to his classroom. In his heart he felt pretty sure that DeWayne had been drunk the night Steffi died. His grandfather covered for him. It was a small, close-knit town. The Pikes were well liked and important. Walter Wilcox was a skinny little vegetable farmer with a daughter driving an old VW. People like that could not be allowed to ruin the promising future of young Pike.

Everybody was talking about the shooting of the man from Florida who had been stalking DeWayne—the man who shot Maya Archer by mistake. Alonee said, "I feel sorry for him. He did a terrible thing hurting Maya, but he must have been mentally ill."

"Yeah," Sami chimed in. "When it first happened I hated that man so much for bringing pain to my little sister. But when I see him on TV lying there so still in the street, I prayed for his soul. You know what Maya said? We didn't want her to see the TV picture of him lying there, but she saw it anyway, and she goes, 'He said he was sorry when he sent me the roses and the money. I bet he told God he was sorry too.' That's what my little sister said. She got no hatred in her heart for that man even though she got that nasty physical therapy and all that. I am so proud of her."

Sereeta looked up from her biology book and said, "All this has been really hard on DeWayne. Imagine having someone sneaking around and trying to shoot you. I don't know how he's been able to study and make good grades with that hanging over his head." Sereeta glanced at Jaris. "And look what that man did to you, kidnapping you when he thought you were DeWayne. That must have been terrifying."

"I bet you were plenty scared then, huh, Jaris?" Derrick Shaw said. "Was the guy really weird?"

Jaris shrugged. He had reported everything to the police, including what he
learned on the Internet. But he didn't go
into details with his friends at school. "It all
happened so fast I didn't have time to
think," he answered. "He was just a guy . . .
an older guy with . . . problems."

"You are one cool cat, Jaris," Sami said.

Jaris glanced over at DeWayne, standing by himself at the beverage machine. He
was staring at Jaris and his friends. He
probably was thinking Jaris was trashing
him to the others. Jaris would have liked to
be doing that, but he told DeWayne he
wouldn't and he planned to keep his word.
Jaris just wanted it all to go away now so
that he wouldn't feel so disgusted every
time he looked at DeWayne Pike.

Jaris walked to English with Alonee. "It
made me so sad when they showed him
lying in the street. They had covered him
but . . . I bet he was one of those people
who've had a sad life. Maybe nothing good
ever happened to him. And then he died

like that," Alonee commented. "Probably he never loved anybody and nobody ever loved him."

Jaris touched Alonee's shoulder, and she turned to him. "Alonee, he had a family. He loved them. He loved them and they loved him. But they are all dead now. He had some good in his life. He was just a guy, Alonee. It all could have been different, but things got crazy and stuff happened. I think sometimes we're all just one bad thing away from some swirling black hole that wants to suck us in."

Alonee looked at Jaris but said nothing. She knew about Jaris's own dark moods. She was probably the only one besides Trevor Jenkins who knew. Jaris's father got down on himself often, and Jaris thought he might have gotten his moods from Pop—the feelings that he would never accomplish anything, that all his dreams would crash like waves on some cruel rocks. A tide of dark green cold water sometimes overwhelmed him, washing over his soul, drowning his spirits. But Jaris always fought his way out of the funks and found something to be grateful for, some light at the end of the tunnel. Yet at times he was desperately afraid that one day that light would go out and he could not make it in the darkness.

As they approached English class, Alonee noted, "Poor Mr. Pippin. Another miserable hour ahead. Those creeps baiting him."

"Yeah, there doesn't seem to be much in Mr. Pippin's life to wave flags over," Jaris remarked. "I guess what keeps him from madness is thinking about retirement. It can't be far off now. I hope he finds some island in the South Seas where there's a nice lady who likes him. I can picture Mr. Pippin, a lei around his neck, dancing barefoot on the beach, a smile on his face. I don't think I've ever seen him smile."

Alonee laughed. "Oh Jaris, wouldn't that be wonderful? He deserves it after our class every day!"

Jaris smiled at Alonee. She was good to be with. No matter how bad he felt, she could always make him feel better. "Want to go for another round of that pineapple pizza after school?" he asked her just before they entered the classroom.

"Yeah, but this time we go dutch," she insisted.

As Mr. Pippin launched into a discussion of the Eudora Welty story, "A Visit of Charity," Marko Lane raised his hand. Mr. Pippin did call on him, but he started speaking anyway. "Hey Mr. Pippin, did you see the old guy killed on TV last night on the news? They blew him away right there on TV. It was awesome."

"No they didn't," another boy chimed in. "We didn't see him get shot. We just saw the dead body."

"We are talking about 'A Visit of Charity,' " Mr. Pippin declared. "I would like to continue the discussion of that. Now the child in the story—Marian—"

"Maybe we could write a story about the old guy who got wasted on TV, Mr. Pippin," Marko suggested. His friends chorused agreement.

"Yeah," a girl added, "that'd be more interesting than this stupid story that I don't even understand."

"It was exciting," another boy said. "I'd like to write about what we saw on TV. Could we?"

"All right!" Mr. Pippin cried in a high-pitched voice, "Enough! You were all supposed to read the Welty story. So now everybody take out a sheet of paper and write a page on the theme of the story. You shall be graded!"

"No fair," cried Marko. "We didn't even read the story yet."

"I assigned it four days ago," Mr. Pippin countered. "I asked you to be ready to discuss it today. Now get out paper and do the writing. I shall collect your papers at the end of class." Mr. Pippin then sat down at his desk. Jaris could see the perspiration shining on the bald center of his head where a few hairs had been carefully combed over.

Jaris had read the story and he had no problem writing about it. Alonee was busily writing too. She always dutifully did her assignments. At the bell, Mr. Pippin scooped up the papers with malicious glee. Half the class turned in blank papers. He held them aloft, crowing, "F! F! F! . . ."

Over pineapple pizza across the street, Alonee told Jaris about her plans for Sereeta's sixteenth birthday. "She's been going through some hard times lately, and I think we all have to put our heads together and do something special so she knows how much we love her," Alonee said.

"That'd be great, Alonee," Jaris responded. "I've been worried about her too."

"I talked it over with Sami," Alonee went on, her eyes shining with excitement "We don't have to spend a lot of money to have a great birthday party. We could have a barbecue, and Trevor and his friends know a DJ who'll work for almost nothing. Sami's uncle lives in a really cool house with a huge backyard, even a little water- fall. There's a nice patio for dancing and we could get a lot of balloons."

"Wow!" Jaris exclaimed. "You guys got it all squared away."

"Well, Sereeta has been acting weird lately. She's not herself. The stuff going on at home, she feels like she doesn't belong anymore. I think she needs to be reminded how much she matters to her friends. I heard somebody say once that friends are the family you choose when your real family doesn't come through," Alonee asserted.

"Sami's uncle is a cop, so we don't have to worry about the party getting out of hand, right?" Jaris asked.

"Actually, he and his wife'll be in Hawaii. It's their twenty-fifth wedding anniversary. Trevor's older brother will be there to keep the lid on. I don't think we have to worry about our friends," Alonee said. "Sami is doing the invitations and she's saying 'No liquor, no drugs,' and anybody who breaks that rule is going to be strangled. And *nobody* crosses Sami!"

Jaris went home in a better mood than when he went to school in the morning. He planned to get Sereeta something really special for her birthday. She loved gold earrings, and they looked beautiful against her honey-brown skin and dark curls. Jaris saw some nice earrings in a jewelry store on sale, well within his budget. He couldn't wait to get them and put them in one of those pretty little satin-lined boxes for Sereeta. Gold earrings would *really* make Sereeta feel special.

Jaris hoped that DeWayne Pike wouldn't come to the birthday party, but he was sure Sami would invite him. Sereeta had dated DeWayne several times, and Sereeta would wonder why he wasn't there. But still, Jaris held out the faint hope that DeWayne would have the decency to stay away, knowing what Jaris knew. But even if DeWayne came, Jaris had no intention of letting his presence spoil Sereeta's party.

Jaris went by the jewelry store and looked at the golden earrings. He didn't have the money for them until payday. He went into the store and asked the clerk if he could put the earrings on hold. He was elated when the clerk agreed.

CHAPTER SEVEN

Jaris worked late at the Chicken Shack, and it was payday that night. At quarter to ten, Mom was there to pick him up. His parents were adamant that he would no longer walk home nights.

When Jaris reached the car, Mom said in a tense voice, "Look, Jaris. Isn't that Shane Burgess hanging around the car wash across the street?"

"Yeah, it looks like him," Jaris admitted, his heart sinking. Poor Ms. McDowell. If Shane was getting into trouble again, it was bad news for her.

"Look, kids are coming up to him," Mom remarked. "Oh Jaris, I think he's dealing drugs over there! I knew Ms. McDowell was making a mistake bringing him back into the neighborhood. I bet he's dealing crack!"

"Wait a minute, Mom. We don't know that," Jaris cautioned. "Just hold on and let me check."

"Jaris," Mom cried, "don't go over there! Don't confront him. He could have a knife or—"

"I won't confront anybody, Mom," Jaris said, heading across to the car wash. He heard his mother's frantic protests in the background. "Jaris, come back here this minute! Do you hear me?"

Cars were going into and out of the car wash, and Shane was standing over to the side. When Jaris got close, he noticed Shane was wearing a T-shirt with something written in pink on it.

"Join the 5K Walk Against Breast Cancer," the message on Shane's shirt read. Shane held a clipboard and he was taking names.

"Hey Shane," Jaris said.

Shane looked a lot different than he

had when Jaris saw him tagging that night near Grant Street. He looked wasted and hostile then. Now he looked friendly. He looked like a different person. "Hey Jaris. Want to take a flyer for the five-kay walk? My sister Torie's going to be in it. We lost our mom to that disease a long time ago. We're walking for her. It's on Saturday morning around the bay."

"Yeah, give me a flyer," Jaris agreed, a big grin breaking on his face. He felt so relieved he wanted to high-five Shane right there. "So Sparky, how's it going?"

"Pretty good. I'm taking classes at home, and I think I'll be in regular school next semester. My sister is helping me a lot," Shane replied.

"She's the best teacher at Tubman High, Shane," Jaris said. "You can ask anybody. She's awesome."

Jaris ran back across the street, where Mom waited anxiously. As he got in beside her, Jaris handed his mother the flyer. "He's passing these out," he told her. "There's a five-kay walk around the bay on Saturday for breast cancer research. He said he and Ms. McDowell's mom died of that years ago. He looks good, Mom. He's really doing well. Ms. McDowell wanted to get her little brother back on the right track, and it looks like she's doing it." He was itching to add, "See, me and Pop were right and you were wrong, Mom," but he didn't dare.

Mom started the car, her jaw set. "Well, I'm very glad it's all working out. I'm happy that Shane isn't in any trouble. But you can't be too careful. It's all well and good to give people second chances, but you have to be sure you're not ruining the lives of good kids in the process. But fine, this time it seems to have worked. I take my hat off to Torie McDowell. She went out on a limb for the boy and it worked." Then Mom added, "I hope. The jury is still out. I hope a year from now Shane is still doing well."

Jaris smiled to himself. Mom did not like to be wrong, but she was a good person. She would rather be proven wrong than to see a kid's life go down the drain.

"Mom," Jaris said on the way home, "we're having a big birthday party for Sereeta at Sami's uncle's house. Sereeta needs a boost. She's been feeling bad because her mom and her stepfather are having a baby, and everybody is so excited about the baby that they're sort of ignoring Sereeta. She feels like an outsider. We want to prove how special she is to her friends."

Mom smiled. "That's nice," she said. "Sereeta is a sweet girl. Very sensitive. I was quite close to her mother, you know. Olivia and I used to go shopping Saturdays. It was quite a routine. She was a lot of fun. I'm sure Olivia cares deeply for Sereeta, but with a new baby coming, there's a lot of hormonal changes. She's about my age, and here she is, like a new bride, expecting a baby. It's a whole new life for her."

Then she looked very serious. "She told me once that her marriage to Tom had been a big mistake. They fell very much in love, but they were never compatible. The longer they were married, the more they realized that. At least Olivia did."

Jaris felt a little nervous. Whenever Mom talked like that, he thought about her and pop. Did she ever regret marrying someone so different from herself? Jaris detected sympathy for Sereeta's mother in her voice. As they neared home, Mom said, "Poor Livy. She *did* try to make it work but . . . "

"Sereeta is in a real bad way," Jaris commented. "The other day she was lying on the grass sobbing."

Mom turned and looked at Jaris. "Poor little thing!" she said. "I hope things get better for her. I should probably call Livy up and remind her to give Sereeta more attention. But we haven't been friends in such a long time. She might resent me calling now after all this time. We had a falling-out, so to speak. We just didn't see things eye to eye anymore. I'm afraid

I can be very judgmental and I shouldn't be. But I've always believed that when you speak those vows before the altar . . . well, come hell or high water, there you are. And Livy . . . well, she doesn't feel that way."

Jaris made no comment, but what his mother said both surprised him and heartened him. He always knew his mother took her marriage vows seriously, but she had not spoken like that before, at least not to Jaris.

When they got home, Pop was not in a very good mood. His basketball team had lost again, but that was not the worst. He had demanded a raise from his boss, Jeremiah Jackson. Jackson said he would think about it, enraging Pop, who believed he deserved an immediate yes. Pop thought Jackson would be so frightened of losing his best employee that he would come through at once to meet Pop's demand.

"That bum," Pop fumed. "He knows I'm the only reason anybody comes in that stinking garage. It's a dirty, messy place, and to make matters worse he keeps a mean-looking bulldog in the office, which does not improve the smell of the place. Jackson has the personality of a rattlesnake. People come in there because I'm a friendly guy, I laugh with the customers, and I fix their beaters. I do it quick and reasonable. Everybody knows that. It's bad enough that all I could accomplish in life is to be a grease monkey, but believe you me, I am going to be a well paid grease monkey, or Jackson can take that job and shove it."

"Oh Lorenzo," Mom responded nervously. "Don't make rash decisions."

"He gives me my raise or I am outta there," Pop asserted.

"Lorenzo, listen to me," Mom insisted. "I have a good job, but we have a lot of bills. We have two kids who will be going to college. We've got a mortgage."

"Don't worry about our financial situation girl," Pop said. "I've always taken care of my family and I always will. When I look in the mirror and see this greasy old coot with the graying hair getting old before his time from inhaling noxious fumes from old beaters, it's bad enough. But I am at least going to be the best paid old greasy coot in town, or Jackson will be looking for another mechanic."

Mom rolled her eyes. She knew better than to argue any further. Arguing only made Pop more determined to have his own way. And, although he had taken the pledge, there was still liquor in the cabinet, and Mom was not totally sure it would stay there if he got frustrated enough.

Mom went into the bathroom and Jaris heard her open the aspirin bottle. When Jaris passed the open bathroom door, he said softly, "Don't worry, Mom. Pop wouldn't really quit his job. He's just shooting off steam."

"He's just stubborn enough to do it, Jaris," Mom countered. She went into the bedroom then and did what she always did when there was a problem with Pop. She called Grandma Jessie. Jaris heard her speaking softly.

"Mom? Yes, again. No, not drinking this time, thank God. But raving about his job. He's threatening to quit the garage if he doesn't get a raise. Yes, he means it. And in this economy. Oh Mom, I have a terrible headache. Yes I know, I know . . ."

Jaris could imagine what Grandma Jessie was saying. "I don't know how you put up with that man and his rages. It's just not right. You poor dear. You deserve better sweetie. Oh darling, didn't I tell you? Didn't I try to warn you? But you were oh so much in love . . . well, let's hope for the best."

After school the next day, Jaris went down to the jewelry shop to buy the gold earrings for Sereeta. He had mixed feelings about his purchase. The more he thought about buying them, the more worried he became. Maybe Sereeta would be confused, even shocked by the gift. After all, they weren't dating. After that first date they had never gone out again. Maybe the gift would embarrass Sereeta. Maybe it was inappropriate.

Jaris did not want to ask his mother about the gift. She would surely advise against it. Mom would point out that such a big gift would be only for someone you were steadily dating.

"Do you have a nice box for these?" Jaris asked. The clerk was a young man only a few years older than Jaris.

"Of course!" the clerk said, producing a lovely little box lined with white satin. It made the gold earrings even more beautiful. When Jaris paid cash for the earrings, he put the box in his backpack and left it there until school the next day.

"Trevor," Jaris confided at lunch, "I need to show you something." He took out the box and opened it.

"Whoa!" Trevor gasped. "That's awesome man."

"For Sereeta, for her birthday," Jaris explained. He looked nervously at Trevor, waiting for an honest reaction. When Trevor didn't say anything, Jaris asked, "Do you think she'll like them?"

"She'll love them man," Trevor said. "But I don't think she's expecting something like this from you. I mean, bro, no offense, but she's not your girlfriend, right?"

"I know, but she knows I care about her," Jaris said defensively. "We had a real good time on that date and . . ."

"It's what you'd give a real girlfriend when you'd been hanging out together for a long time, bro," Trevor insisted. "How many karats in that puppy man?"

"Ten," Jaris answered. "It was marked down. It used to be almost a hundred dollars, but it was marked down."

"Well, it's a great gift man," Trevor said.

"But you think I'm making a big mistake giving her something like this, don't you? You think I'm making a fool of myself," Jaris groaned.

Trevor shrugged. "Listen man," he told Jaris, "I'm no expert on girls. Maybe she'll be so blown away, she'll want to go with you more. You gotta do what your heart tells you man. You hear what I'm saying?"

"Yeah," Jaris replied, holding the little box in the palm of his hand. He stared at the earrings. "They're so beautiful," he said, "like her."

Jaris didn't tell anybody else about his special gift for Sereeta. It was one of the things he could share only with Trevor, who would keep quiet about it and not ridicule Jaris over it or even tease him. The expression on Trevor's face told Jaris how he felt about the gift. He thought it was way over the top for somebody not even in a relationship. But he wouldn't come right out and be forceful about it. He'd just hint at what he had to say. But if Jaris had told Sami, she would have exploded in laughter and said, "Boy, you being a big fool, you know it? You take that box back right now and get your money back. You give that girl a box of candy or a little stuffed animal. No way you need to be giving her gold earrings. Dude, are you crazy? She is going to think you have lost your mind."

In the meantime, Jaris, Chelsea, and Mom were dreading Monday. Pop was more determined than ever to have a showdown with Jackson. He would go to work early, and, if he didn't get his raise, he would come home. That was the plan.

"I am little enough of a man already for giving up on all my dreams I had as a young man," Pop intoned in his deep voice. "I settled for being a grease monkey."

Pop had an exceptionally good breakfast to fortify himself for the battle ahead. He had an extra helping of pancakes, sausage, bacon, and oatmeal. "I am asking the man right off and, if he says no, I am out of there because I will not work for that skinflint!"

"Lorenzo, he already pays you very well," Mom groaned. "I don't know of another mechanic who earns as much as you do."

"But I'm worth more, lady," Pop insisted. "I'm the backbone of his business. I am the man."

They watched him march out to his pickup truck and get in. He revved up the engine and was gone down the street. It was still early. Jackson always got there early and had his coffee before he opened the garage. The garage was only a few blocks from the Spain home, so if things did not work out, Pop would be home before Mom or Jaris or Chelsea had to go to school.

Mom stood at the window like a statue. "I have another splitting headache," she groaned.

The green pickup appeared at the end of the street. "Oh my Lord," Mom cried. "He's coming home! He didn't get it. Oh my Lord, he has quit his job. That crazy man has quit his job. Your father has gone mad!"

Jaris wanted to say it was okay but he couldn't, because it wasn't.

CHAPTER EIGHT

Pop jumped from the pickup. He came in the house and looked at his family. "That no good skinflint looks at me like I have lost my mind for asking for more money. He goes, 'Spain, do you think I'm made of money? I got expenses. I got overhead.' I go, 'Take it or leave it. You know the kind of money I want.' And he gives it to me! Everything I ask for!" A huge grin broke out on Pop's face. He grabbed Mom and swung her around as if she weighed no more than a feather. "You mighta married a grease monkey, baby, but you didn't marry a wimp! You hear what I'm saying?"

"Lorenzo Spain, I could kill you!" Mom scolded.

Pop looked at Jaris and Chelsea. "You kids. Listen up," he demanded. "You are my witnesses. The woman is wanting to kill me. When they find my body on the kitchen floor with a steak knife in my back, you know who did it."

Mom started laughing. Happy tears ran down her face. It was like the night Jaris won the role of Sydney Carton in *A Tale of Two Cities*. Mom and Pop danced across the school parking lot like wild children. And now they danced around the kitchen, knocking over pots and pans.

Pop went back to Jackson's, and Jaris went to school encouraged. Pop took a risk, a big risk—and it paid off. He was getting more respect and more money in his paycheck. It was a risk to give Sereeta the gold earrings, but it was a risk worth taking. She would finally know how much she meant to Jaris.

When Jaris walked into American history, he saw DeWayne Pike leaning over Sereeta's desk. They were both smiling.

Jaris felt resentment boiling inside him. He knew DeWayne liked Sereeta and had dated her a few times, but out of respect for that dead girl in Florida, Jaris thought he ought to cool his social life. After all, Steffi's father hadn't even been buried yet! Jaris couldn't understand why DeWayne at least didn't feel some guilt. Why didn't he give it some time before moving in on Sereeta?

Jaris sat down at his desk. It crossed his mind to tell Sereeta the whole story. He told DeWayne he would not tell anybody, but maybe that had been a foolish promise. Didn't Sereeta have the right to know the kind of guy who was coming on to her? Didn't she deserve to know about Steffi and how the lost blood sample made it impossible to prove DeWayne's guilt?

Jaris sank deeper into his seat. Would he be telling Sereeta the whole story because she had a right to know or to get rid of a rival? Because he could not answer that question, Jaris said nothing.

For the past several days, Ms. McDowell had been showing news coverage of the Vietnam War protests and playing the protest music from singers like Bob Dylan. Now she started a discussion of the issue. "Why do you think the antiwar movement was so widespread and passionate during the nineteen-sixties and seventies?" she asked.

"Because of the news coverage," Jaris answered. "My grandmother told me that her family watched Walter Cronkite on CBS every night. They would show the injured American soldiers being taken to helicopters. They showed the injured Vietnamese civilians, like one little girl running down the road on fire from the bombing. The war came right into peoples' living rooms, and they saw how bad it was, and they wanted to stop it."

"Yes, that made a big difference," Ms. McDowell agreed. "In earlier wars, the civilians saw very little of the actual war. There were newsreels of captured soldiers and bombed-out cities, but the coverage was closely controlled by the military. Was that a good thing or a bad thing?"

A girl raised her hand. "My grandpa told me we lost that war because the newspeople made everything look hopeless," she reported. "My grandpa said the news guys should be kept away from wars so the military can do what it has to do."

"Well," Ms. McDowell commented, "that's what happens when you live in a democracy like the United States. It's a constant struggle between national security and free speech."

Sereeta spoke up then. "I think truth is too important to ever cover up," she said. "The American people had to be told the truth about the war."

Jaris thought he *should* tell Sereeta about DeWayne's past. Didn't she just say truth was too important to cover up? He should lay it all out for her, and then she could decide if she still wanted to date DeWayne.

Jaris left class right after Sereeta. As usual, he admired the beautiful contour of her cheeks and dark curls. He imagined the gold earrings on her ears. When they got beyond the crowd, he would draw her over to a private place to tell her about DeWayne. He would be very calm about it so that she wouldn't suspect he had his own motives for revealing the information. He would even tell her that her comment about the Vietnam War coverage made up his mind to tell her.

"Hi Sereeta," Jaris said. "How's everything?"

Sereeta shrugged. That sad look was still in her eyes. Apparently things had not improved at home.

"Sereeta, can I talk to you for a minute?" Jaris asked. His heart was pounding. His gut was telling him this was the wrong thing to do. He had framed the words he would use in his mind. He had even rehearsed them, like he rehearsed Sydney Carton's lines in the play. But when they stood alone under the eucalyptus tree, the words would not come together and pass through Jaris's lips.

It was wrong, Jaris thought. It was wrong to tell Sereeta or anybody when he promised DeWayne he wouldn't.

"Sereeta, want to go to a movie or something this weekend?" Jaris asked her instead.

Sereeta shook her head. "I don't want to go to a movie. Maybe we could go to some little club where the music is really blasting. I want really loud drums. I'd want the music to blast so loud that the ceiling would seem to lift up. I'd want the music to make my brain tremble. Do you know a place like that, Jaris?" Sereeta asked.

"Yeah," Jaris answered. "My friend Trevor goes to the Bitter Python Room. The music is a mix of rap and rock. It's really loud."

"Yeah, that'd be good," Sereeta said. "Right now I'm into rap. The angrier the better. I want the lyrics to crash into my brain and fill up all the crevices and drown all my thoughts."

Jaris spent the rest of the day worrying about Sereeta. At lunch he talked to Alonee and Sami about it. "Sereeta seems so . . ."

"Weird," Sami finally filled in the word. "I'm tellin' you, that child is in trouble. She don't even eat her lunch no more. She already looks like a stick, and now she don't eat? 'You wanna disappear from this earth, girl?' I ask her, and she like gives me this crazy smile like that's just what she'd like to do."

Alonee nodded. "I've tried to tell her that after the baby comes," she said, "things will settle down to normal. The baby won't be such a big deal when he's crying at two in the morning and needing a diaper change every ten minutes. I even tried telling her the baby is her half brother and maybe even she'll bond with him. Boy was *that* a mistake. She told me the baby has nothing to do with her and never will."

"That birthday party might be just the right thing to snap her out of the bad mood she's in,"

Jaris said hopefully. "When she sees how much she means to all of us, she's bound to feel better."

"Yeah, that's what I'm hoping," Sami said.

When Tommy Jenkins, Trevor's older brother, drove Jaris and Sereeta to the Bitter Python, he said, "They got the hottest music in town." He smiled at Sereeta and said, "If you want it ballistic, you got it."

The club was tucked between a used furniture store and a bowling alley. The musicians were setting up on stage, and already the room was crowded. From the outside, the place looked small, but inside it was cavernous. "They got groups just starting out," Tommy said, "just getting some attention. It's the kind of place you woulda seen Kanye West and Outkast before they hit the big time. You come in here and it's happening. You can just feel the vibes."

Tommy left Jaris and Sereeta to join some friends then. Sereeta said wryly,

"My mother hates this kind of music. When I was little, she made me take piano lessons. I hated them so much. But I took them to make her happy. I knew something was wrong at our house, and I thought if I did everything to make Mom happy maybe I could fix whatever it was. But it didn't work. Turns out I couldn't make her happy. I love music just as wild and loud as it gets. My first favorite song was 'Born to be Wild.' I listened to that over and over. It was just amazing. I could feel the vibrations going right through me. I could be all tense and angry, and all that feeling drained out of me through that music."

The birthday party was one week away. Jaris wished it was even sooner. He thought about the gold earrings and tried to plan the best time and place to give them to her. Maybe just when the party was ending. He'd take her outside, by the little waterfall. He didn't want his precious gift just piled on the table with all the other birthday gifts.

"Yes," Jaris thought, "I'll bring her to the little waterfall." He had been to Sami's uncle's house several times, and that was the most beautiful and secluded spot. It would be just the two of them standing there, and he would put the little white box in her hands. He could see, when she saw the earrings, her beautiful, expressive eyes opening wider than they had ever opened. She'd probably tell him he shouldn't have spent so much money on the gift, but she wouldn't really mean that because she'd be so happy with it. She might even shed happy tears, not like the bitter tears she shed on the school lawn that day.

The groups who came on stage were loud and original. As they banged on their drums and screamed their lyrics, Sereeta seemed absorbed. Jaris was glad if she was getting some comfort from the music. Perspiration poured from the faces of the performers. One young man, who went by the name of Ask an Asp, shouted out his rap like he was mad at the world. Sereeta turned to Jaris and confided, "Sometimes you feel like that. You're not supposed to, but you do. We're supposed to be okay with everything that happens, but we're not . . ."

When Tommy dropped Sereeta at her house, she asked Jaris to come in for a few minutes. "They're home," she told him. "I know you've met my mother. She and your Mom went shopping when we were in middle school. My stepfather will be in the den on the computer."

Jaris stepped into the front room with Sereeta, and he saw a very beautiful woman he knew before as Olivia Prince. He remembered her and his mom rushing off to the mall every Saturday like teenagers. That seemed really long ago. Even back then, Jaris remembered thinking Sereeta got her beauty from her mother.

"Mom," Sereeta said, "this is Jaris. I told you about Jaris. He's in my American history class."

Olivia Manley, the woman's new name since she remarried, looked at Jaris and said, "You're Monie's son, aren't you? My, you've grown so tall. You're a young man now. I haven't seen you in a long time. How are your brothers?"

Jaris wasn't sure what to say. "My sister, Chelsea, she's fine," he finally said.

Olivia Manley looked puzzled. She took a sip from a goblet filled with a yellow-green liquid—a margarita. "I thought Monie had three sons," she said. "Well, it's nice to see you again, Jack."

"Yeah," Jaris replied, as the woman turned and filled her glass again from a yellow-green bottle.

Jaris kissed Sereeta good-bye. She had tears in her eyes.

"Get your goodnight kiss from the babe bro?" Tommy asked when Jaris climbed in beside him.

"Yeah," Jaris said.

"You don't sound too happy. That girl is mega hot," Tommy remarked.

"Her mom was drinking alcohol and already she's wasted. She's gonna have a baby and she's drinking like that," Jaris said.

"Her business man," Tommy said. "We're not in charge of the world."

"She didn't even remember my name. She called me Jack," Jaris went on. "She asked me how my brothers were. She and Mom went shopping every weekend, and she doesn't remember *anything*."

"Dude, she doesn't *care*. She's into her own stuff," Tommy said.

"Yeah, that's why she can't even see that her daughter is falling apart," Jaris said bitterly.

Tommy shrugged. "Not all mothers can be like mine man," Tommy said. "Maybe that's a good thing. The world couldn't handle many more Mickey Jenkinses. Mom is like a drill sergeant, and Trevor and me and our older brothers are her platoon. Every day she made sure we brushed our teeth, combed our hair, got all our homework done. You know, my oldest brother, Desmond, he told me that boot camp was a piece of cake. He said his sarge was a pussycat compared to Mom."

"Proves she loves you guys," Jaris said.

Tommy nodded. "I know man, but it ain't always easy when you're held on too tight a leash," he responded. "You sometimes think you're choking, know what I'm saying?"

The birthday party for Sereeta was scheduled for a Saturday night ten days before Sereeta's actual birthday. Sami thought that this way she would never guess something was afoot. On the Monday before the party, Sami approached Sereeta and said, "Girl, we're having a party for my uncle. A big surprise party. He's a police officer, you know, and he got an important anniversary coming up. Twenty years on the force. We having a big shindig. He helped a lot of kids, so we all gonna be there. Be a lotta fun. You can come, right, Sereeta?"

"Sure, I'll come," Sereeta replied.

CHAPTER NINE

On the Monday before the Saturday night party, all Sereeta's friends got together after school at Trevor's house to make the final plans for the party. Jaris was sorry to see that DeWayne was part of the group. Jaris had hoped that somehow DeWayne would decide not to come, but that was hoping for too much.

"We got the helium tank to inflate the balloons," Sami announced. "Gonna be lots of balloons in Sereeta's favorite color—red. We got all the streamers. They gonna be hanging from the trees outside. We got the DJ lined up. He's cool. We're gonna have barbecue and pizza and burgers, plenty of sodas. My mama is the best cake baker in the world, and she is gonna make an awe-some cake. Main thing, we gotta all bring cards and write real warm stuff there, full of love for our birthday girl. The gifts, they don't need to be more than little things. That's not what this party is about, hear what I'm tellin' you?"

Jaris felt a little nervous. He was going overboard on his gift. He didn't want to make everybody else feel bad.

"Everybody just bring some little token gifts—lotions, sweet-smelling soaps, cookies, candy, whatever. But those cards—Sereeta gotta read the love there," Sami demanded.

Jaris decided he would buy some cheap little gift and put it on the pile with the others on the table. Maybe he'd buy Sereeta a pretty little mirror for her purse. Then, when nobody was looking, he'd slip her the gold earrings out by the waterfall. Nobody would need to know except for Jaris and Sereeta.

"I asked Ms. McDowell if Shane would like to come," Sami said, "and she was touched that we'd think to include him,

so he's coming too. We won't say nothin'
to anybody about that. Everybody be nice
to Shane 'cause he's got a high mountain to
climb right now."

"You bet," Alonee agreed.

"My brother Tommy will pick up Sereeta
and take her home," Trevor chimed in.

Jaris was happy that the plans for the
party were turning out well. The only sour
note was DeWayne being there, but Jaris
resolved to be polite to him. Jaris wanted
nothing to spoil Sereeta's party. He was
hoping this would be just what she needed
to climb out of the despair she was feeling.
Like Alonee had said, it was up to the
friends who loved you to fill in when your
own family came up short.

At school on Tuesday, Marko Lane
came over to Jaris and probed. "I'm getting a
buzz that you guys are planning something.
Some big hush-hush party coming up?"

Jaris didn't want to deny that anything was
underway because then Marko would keep
on digging until he came onto something.

The last thing they needed was Marko and his creepy friends crashing Sereeta's party and ruining everything. "Well, since you found out anyway, we're having a final party for the cast of *A Tale of Two Cities*," Jaris said. "It's just for the cast and kids who worked on the play. We're having a pizza party in the auditorium after school in two weeks. But don't be hanging around, Marko. It's very uncool to come to a party you're not invited to."

Marko sneered. "Hey man, I wouldn't dream of crashing your stupid party. What kind of guy do you think I am?" He walked off, snickering. Jaris smiled to himself. Two weeks from now, Marko and his friends would find out he'd been tricked, but Sereeta's party would have been saved.

Right after school on Friday, Trevor, Jaris, Derrick, and DeWayne went over to Sami's uncle's house to get some of the decorations in place. They hung lights from the trees and shrubs outside. Jaris took a special look at the little waterfall. He and

DeWayne hung the large banner that read "Happy Birthday Sereeta!" For a few moments, as they worked together mounting the bulky banner, Jaris forgot how he felt about DeWayne. Jaris kept telling himself he had to be nice to DeWayne for Sereeta's sake.

"Lookin' awesome, boys!" Sami exclaimed, clapping in approval. "Come look at the cake Mama made. It's in the fridge."

Everybody took a peek at the three-tiered white cake with Sereeta's name in red frosting.

"Sereeta hasn't the vaguest idea of what we're doing," Alonee said. "She's just going to freak!"

Derrick came up to Jaris and asked softly, "Look, I just got a little perfume for her. You think that's enough? I got it at the drugstore."

"That's great, Derrick," Jaris assured him.

"You think?" Derrick asked with a smile.

"Okay," Sami said, "last-minute drill. Everybody has to be here tomorrow by six. Tommy's gonna get Sereeta and bring her here at six thirty. We all gonna be positioned around, and we see her and we start singing the happy birthday song."

Jaris wrapped his little fake jewel mirror with gift paper and added it to the pile already on the table. Sereeta would think this was his gift. Later on, by the waterfall, the big moment would come—at the end of the party. Just the thought of it made goose bumps pop out on Jaris's arms.

At home around midday on Saturday, Jaris happened to hear a news report on the radio. He was waiting for the sports scores when it came on.

Police have finished their preliminary report on the death of Walter Wilcox, the Florida man who led the police on a chase before being shot near Tubman High. The shooting by the police has been ruled justified. Wilcox was holding a gun in his hand when he stepped from the car, and he refused to put it down. Wilcox has no next of kin, but his body has been claimed by the Florida chapter of Parents of Drunk Driving Victims, or PDD. Candice Ash, spokesperson for the group, said they did not want this man's remains placed in a pauper's grave. His ashes will be returned to Florida and interred with those of his wife and daughter, Stephanie, allegedly the victim of a drunk driver.

Jaris felt as if someone had hit him in the face with a wet towel, and DeWayne's lies all came rushing back into his mind, sickening him. The system had failed Walter Wilcox in life, but at least he would have a dignified burial.

Later that day, at the house of Sami's uncle, the first of the Tubman High students arriving were Trevor and Derrick. Jaris was next. Sami put them to work hanging the streamers.

"I'm so hungry I could start eating right now," Trevor complained.

"Don't you even think of touching the food, dude, or I'll have your head," Sami laughed.

Many of the students were dropped off by their parents. Alonee's mother brought her. Another van brought several more boys and girls, including Shane. DeWayne arrived, driving an almost brand-new silver Honda.

The big room filled up quickly. There were about twenty-five people in the room as Sereeta's arrival loomed. Tommy left the Archer house in his old Chevrolet Cavalier at six-twenty. He promised to bring Sereeta back at six-thirty sharp.

"I could have picked up Sereeta in my car," DeWayne had said to Tommy. "It's a lot classier than your old heap, Tommy. It's a shame the birthday girl has to ride in a rust bucket when she could ride in my nice car."

Jaris fought the anger boiling inside him. "DeWayne," Jaris said, "you and I are the same age. We've got just provisional licenses. The rules are we can't drive anyone under the age of twenty. You couldn't legally bring Sereeta. Tommy's over twenty-one."

DeWayne smiled. "Hey dude, don't get your drawers in a knot. This is just a few blocks to and from the girl's house. Who's going to be watching? Who's going to care? I just thought Sereeta deserved to come to her party in a phat ride," DeWayne said.

"She'll be fine," Jaris snapped. He walked quickly away from DeWayne. He knew if he stayed a minute longer, he would say something he would regret. Hearing that news story about Walter Wilcox opened up the old wounds.

"Jaris," Sami advised, "I put on all the invites no alcohol. Not one drop. I don't think we got anything to worry about, but keep your eyes open. If you see anybody spiking the punch or anything, we're gonna throw them out on their ears in two seconds, okay?"

Jaris nodded.

"You guys!" screamed Alonee. "I see Tommy turning the corner. He's coming down the street. Sereeta's with him. You guys! Get ready to scream. . . . She's almost here. . . . He's parking. . . . She's getting out . . . three-two-one—"

CHAPTER TEN

Everybody was gathered in a semicircle. As Tommy opened the door and ushered Sereeta in, the voices exploded in happy birthdays. "Happy birthday dear Sereeta, happy birthday to you!" Alonee had been clutching the red balloons and now they bobbed in a festive rush to the high ceiling. The huge banner with Sereeta's name on it glowed with lights on the wall. The streamers floated in the air, encouraged by fans.

Sereeta stood there looking stunned for a minute. Then she gasped. "You guys!" she cried. "You guys! I don't believe this. This isn't happening. On my—you guys!" Tears ran down her face. She wiped away the tears and glanced at the balloons on the ceiling, at the dancing streamers. "I can't believe this. I just can't believe this," Sereeta kept saying over and over.

Everybody rushed to Sereeta for a hug. She was surrounded by her friends' arms as the aroma of barbecued chicken, grilled burgers, and hot pizza floated from the backyard, where more balloons and streamers waited.

Everybody went into the backyard for the food. Sami nudged Jaris and whispered, "That girl hasn't eaten a good meal in a month, and look at her loading her plate with two chicken legs, a big slice of pizza, and a burger!"

Jaris smiled happily as Sereeta dug into the food. They scooped out pink lemonade from the punch bowls and popped cans of ginger ale. Then the DJ arrived, and music started booming from the living room— rock and rap, as loud as Sereeta liked it.

Sereeta gathered everybody at the table where the gifts were piled, and she opened each one, raving over the smallest trifle as if it was the most desired gift she had ever received. She read the notes aloud and cried again and laughed. Then Sereeta declared, "Nobody in the whole world has better friends than I do. I mean, I'm telling you guys, you are the greatest friends in the world. To think you would do something like this for me. I never in a million years dreamed you'd do something like this for me." Sereeta cried again, but she cried happy tears, not sad ones. Jaris had never seen her looking more beautiful and radiant.

Sereeta hugged everybody, one by one, including Jaris, but he was waiting for the moment by the waterfall. That would make this unforgettable night even more awesome for Sereeta.

"We're going to cut the cake now," Sami announced. She leaned over to Jaris and said, "Everything cool, huh? Nobody misbehavin'?"

"Roger!" Jaris reported with a big smile.

Sereeta did the honors of cutting the cake. Sami insisted on Sereeta's taking the first piece, the one with her name on it. "Oh," Sereeta sighed, "this is the best cake I ever tasted. It's so moist and creamy!"

"Nothin' but the best for the best," Sami said.

Most of those who came to the party danced on the big outdoor patio to the DJ's music. Jaris hated to see Sereeta dancing with DeWayne, but then Jaris got his own turn. It felt so good to have Sereeta in his arms. He couldn't think of a happier moment in his life.

It was getting late. The plan was to end the party at eleven so that everybody could get home safely. Tommy came alongside Sami and said, "I can take the birthday girl home anytime. I've already loaded her gifts in the car."

"Sereeta!" Sami called out, "Tommy's ready to take you home girl."

"Sereeta!" Alonee called out to her too. "I saw her a minute ago."

"Sereeta!" Jaris called out in his strong baritone voice.

"Maybe she went to the little girl's room," Alonee suggested. "I'll check." Alonee ran to the two bathrooms and found both empty.

Then Derrick approached Jaris. He had a worried look on his face. "DeWayne wanted to show her his new car," Derrick said. "He kept talking about the cool interior, all the padding and stuff. He said the dashboard was like an instrument panel in a jet or something."

"Did anybody see Sereeta leave?" Jaris yelled.

"I saw her go outside with that guy who played Charles Darnay in the play," a girl replied. "They were laughing."

Ice water ran down Jaris's spine. He pushed through the crowd of students and rushed outside. "Sereeta!" he yelled. He thought she'd be standing with DeWayne alongside his Honda. But the Honda was gone. There was no sign of Sereeta or of DeWayne.

"Oh my God," Jaris gasped to the others who had spilled outside with him. He saw something glittering in the shrubs near where the Honda had been parked. It was a bottle of whisky. It had been drained. "That slime! He brought booze," Jaris said out loud. Then he thought, "He drank enough to give him the guts to pull this lousy stunt. He's out there with Sereeta."

"He's *driving drunk!*" he yelled.

Tommy jumped into his Cavalier, and Jaris, Trevor, Sami, and Alonee piled in with him. They drove slowly down the winding road where the Archer house stood. No cars were on the road.

"There's a little hill off to the left," Jaris said, "sort of a lover's lane. You can see the lights of the city from there."

"I'll try it," Tommy said, turning onto the twisty dirt road. They got to the top of the hill but no one was there. Tommy drove back down.

Jaris had a pounding headache. He thought his head would split open. Terror clawed at his insides. "DeWayne," he said to himself, "is like he was the night in Florida when he killed Steffi. Only now Sereeta's life is on the line!"

"Let's try the freeway," Tommy said.

"Oh my God!" Jaris exclaimed, "don't let them be on the freeway!"

"He probably told the girl he'd just ride to the end of the street, and then it was too late," Sami groaned. "He showing off what a big man he is!"

Tommy drove onto the freeway, which was crowded with weekend drivers. Tommy had his radio on. Immediately they heard a frightening traffic alert.

"There is a report of a silver Honda driving erratically in the fast lane of the freeway. California Highway Patrol is on the way—that is a silver Honda."

When the freeway was identified, Tommy said, "That's where we are."

Jaris grabbed his cell phone and dialed 9-1-1. "The guy in the silver Honda is drunk," Jaris yelled into the phone. "He's drunk and there's a girl with him!" The 9-1-1 responder thanked him, took his name, and told him the information had been relayed to the authorities.

Terror and guilt flooded Jaris's mind as he hung up. He should have warned Sereeta. He should have told her about Steffi and how she died. When Sereeta saw that DeWayne wasn't going just to the end of the street, did she protest? Did she scream? Or, in the high spirits of the evening, did she think it was okay?

A new, terse traffic report came on the radio.

"There has been a four-car collision on the I-5, near the twenty-four off-ramp. A silver Honda has rear-ended another car, which piled into two more vehicles.

Emergency vehicles are on the way. Avoid this area."

Tommy came up on the accident, though not near enough to see anything but glowing emergency lights flashing in the darkness. Police and fire sirens wailed madly, making the night surreal. "We can't get any closer man," Tommy said.

Trevor reached over and put his arms around Jaris, "It's okay man . . . I don't see any fire . . . it'll be okay . . . take it easy," he said to his close friend.

The four of them arrived at the emergency room soon after the ambulances brought in the injured.

Jaris texted Alonee at the party and told her to let everyone know what happened. Jaris said he and the others would stay at the hospital until there was word.

Olivia Manley came rushing into the hospital waiting room a bit later. DeWayne's parents then arrived, along with family of the other victims. Jaris heard the doctor telling DeWayne's parents that their son was seriously hurt but that he had surviv-able injuries. Another driver was in critical condition.

It seemed like forever before another doctor came to talk to Olivia Manley. Jaris and his friends stood with her. "Sereeta has suffered a concussion and some bruising. She will be all right," said the doctor.

The door to the emergency visitors lounge opened, and Jaris saw Pop come barging in. "Alonee called and told us," Pop declared. He gave Jaris a big hug. Then he shook his head with a look of total disgust. "He did it again. Lord in Heaven! He did it again," Pop sighed.

When it was confirmed that Sereeta was all right, everybody went home except Jaris and his father. Olivia Manley saw her daughter and promised to return in the morning. She explained that her husband insisted on taking her home because she was so close to delivering the baby.

Jaris finally got permission to go into the little cubicle where Sereeta lay on a bed, her head bandaged. Pop waited outside for him.

"Sereeta, I'm so glad you're gonna be okay," Jaris whispered.

"Oh Jaris, I'm sorry. It was such a beautiful party, and I ruined everything. DeWayne said he'd just drive a few feet, but then he took off . . . I'm so sorry," Sereeta sobbed.

"It's not your fault, Sereeta," Jaris assured her. "It's DeWayne's fault for driving drunk. It's my fault for not warning you that he did it before and killed a girl. I should have warned you."

"He killed a girl?" Sereeta asked softly.

"I'll tell you about it when you're better," Jaris quieted her.

Then Jaris gently took Sereeta's hand and placed the little white box into it.

"Jaris!" she whispered.

Jaris opened it for her so that she could see the gold earrings. "I wanted to take you to the little waterfall after the party and give you my real gift there," he said.

Sereeta's hands were trembling as she took the gold earrings. Then she lay them down and reached for Jaris. She brought him down to her and kissed him with lips that were bruised and bleeding. She caressed his hair. She was crying and her lips were quivering. "I love you," she whispered to him. "Jaris, I love you."

He had felt guilty about not telling her about DeWayne, and things almost ended in disaster. Now, he felt, all those shadows of guilt were gone. Sereeta was okay, and she loved him, as he loved her.